NOT THE MARRYING KIND

NICOLA MARSH

Who said marriage had to be convenient?

LA party planner Poppy Collins has kept her side business—planning divorce parties as the Divorce Diva—under wraps, but keeping her sister's company afloat is proving tougher by the day. When a new divorce party prospect gives Poppy the opportunity to save the day and boost her bottom line, she can't pass it up. But this time, she's about to get way more than she bargained for...

Vegas golden boy Beck Blackwood knows Poppy's secret, and he's not afraid to use it to get exactly what he wants—a wife. With his reputation and corporate expansion plans on the line, the only way he can repair the damage is by getting hitched, and fast. And if blackmail is the only way to get Poppy to the altar, then so be it...

But they're in the city of high stakes, and Poppy has a few aces up her sleeve. Now it's time to find out if they're playing to win...or if they're playing for keeps.

Copyright © Nicola Marsh 2012
Published by Nicola Marsh 2017

All the characters, names, places and incidents in this book have no existence outside the imagination of the author and have no relation whatsoever to anyone bearing the same name or names and are used fictitiously. They're not distantly inspired by any individual known or unknown to the author and all the incidents in the book are pure invention. Any resemblance to actual events, locales, or persons, living or dead, is coincidental.

All rights reserved including the right of reproduction in any form. The text or any part of the publication may not be reproduced or transmitted in any form without the written permission of the publisher.

The author acknowledges the copyrighted or trademarked status and trademark owners of the word marks mentioned in this work of fiction.

(Originally published under the same title by Entangled Publishing in July 2012.)

ONE

Divorce Diva Daily recommends:
Playlist: "I Will Survive" by Gloria Gaynor
Movie: He's Just Not That into You
Cocktail: Slow, Comfortable Screw

Beck Blackwood could kill them.

Every one of those uptight, conservative pricks. Beck's fingers curled into fists as he paced his office, oblivious to the million-dollar view of the Strip. He liked his office perched on the highest floor of the tallest tower in Vegas. King of the world. No other feeling beat it. Apart from sex, but he'd even given up on that while finagling every detail of this deal.

This deal... He stopped in front of his desk and slammed his fist against the prospectus, the pain not registering half as much as having a boardroom of investors hedge around his win-win deal because his company wasn't respectable enough. Translation: he wasn't respectable enough. Damn it, he thought he'd left his past behind.

He'd thought wrong. Didn't matter he rivaled the richest guys in town for penthouse space, property investments, and fast cars. Because of his lifestyle choices—single, heterosexual guy who enjoyed his freedom—and the City of Sin he chose to live in, they didn't deem him worthy. Throw in the PR disaster when his site manager was found in a compromising position with an apprentice on one of his prominent constructions recently, and the fate of Blackwood Enterprises had been sealed.

Vegas loved a scandal. Sex between a married guy and a barely eighteen-year-old girl? The press attacked. Every newspaper article had shown his building site, with his company's name boldly emblazoned with its signature cactus. Damned if the thing didn't add a phallic connotation to every word printed.

Never mind he'd fired the manager and set up counseling for the teenager if she needed it.

Never mind he'd been working his ass off trying to recoup losses the company had sustained in the crash of 2020.

Never mind he'd spent the last eighteen months living and breathing this deal to build hotels across the country that would see company profit margins soar again.

Blackwood Enterprises had been crucified. All his hard work down the toilet because they didn't deem him good enough.

Fuck them. He'd sat in the boardroom after presenting projected statistics that would've had guys with half a brain salivating, rage simmering, as each and every one of the pompous bastards scrambled for excuses.

Too big a risk. People are still talking about your

company, and not in a good way.

The face of this project needs to have solid family values. What they were basically saying was that because one of his employees screwed up and he didn't have a band on his ring finger, he wasn't good enough.

Bullshit. His intercom buzzed and he glared at it, not in the mood for interruptions, not in the mood for anything unless it involved eight signatures on the construction deal of a lifetime.

"What is it, Simone?"

"Mr. Robinson wanted to remind you about the function you're planning."

He bit back his first response—*Screw Lou.* "Tell him I'm on it."

"Will do, Mr. Blackwood."

"And I'm incommunicado for the next hour." It'd take him that long to calm down.

"Okay." The intercom fell silent and he flung himself into a chair, ready to tackle a stack of quotes. However, the requisite quick glance at his inbox stalled when he glimpsed an email, every word from Stan Walkerville punctuating his disillusionment at losing out on the deal of the century.

Beck's gut twisted. Stan, the unofficial appointed leader of the investors he'd been counting on earlier today, reiterated his disappointment they wouldn't be building the biggest chain of hotels America had ever seen.

Not half as disappointed as he was. The fortune he'd amassed meant jack if they didn't consider him reliable enough. What did the old farts expect, for him to marry to become the biggest name in construction in the country?

Frigging great, he was back to this. His foolhardy plan. It had first come to him in the meeting when the investors were delivering their verdict because of the tainted Blackwood name. He'd wanted to yell, *What the fuck do you expect me to do, pull a wife out of my ass for respectability?*

While he'd wisely kept his temper in check at the time, the dumb idea had stuck in his head like a burr, no matter how many times he dismissed it. Stupid thing was, he'd analyzed it from every angle and he kept coming back to it. He needed instant propriety to clear his company's name and get the investors on his side again.

A wife would do that. *Shit*. He re-read the email. Twice. Focused on the last line. *If circumstances change, call us. We'd love to do business.* Was it as simple as that? Get hitched? Become the best in the business? Make his dream of being the biggest in America come true?

Only one problem. Where the hell was he going to find a wife? Hating what an idiot he was for even considering getting married for business, Beck scanned the rest of the emails, eventually finding the one he was searching for.

Late last night he'd agreed to another outlandish idea. Lou Robinson, his Chief Financial Officer and oldest friend, had latched onto a crazy idea to throw a party to celebrate Lou's divorce. Worse, in an effort to get Lou refocused on the job and to ensure word didn't get out his company was promoting divorce—another black mark against it for sure—Beck had said he'd organize it. Anything to snap the usually astute CFO out of his crappy mood.

Besides, planning some senseless party had to be better than punching the wall. It'd take his mind off the deal long enough for him to come up with a viable solution for Stan and Co. to quit stalling and sign. One that didn't involve shackling himself to a woman. He grimaced at the thought and as the crisp website in fuchsia font came up, he wrinkled his nose.

Divorce Diva Daily. Apart from some nifty alliteration,

he had a feeling this site offered nothing but a few party favors at an exorbitant price. Not that he objected to Lou spending a fortune on exorcising his demons. Hell, he'd chip in, no matter how much it took. The faster he threw this party, the faster he could have his competent CFO back.

Beck had an agenda. Schedule a meeting with the probable charlatan running this site, plan the party, make sure Lou was back on the job Monday. To come up with a feasible Plan B to wow the investors, he needed his friend alert and focused, two things he hadn't been able to attribute to Lou in a while. Lou needed to get drunk and get laid. He'd latched onto this lame-ass party idea instead. Whatever. If a divorce party would get Lou back on track, Beck was all for it. The faster he could get this happening, the better.

Against his better judgment, he started reading the diva's blog entry for today.

Top Tips for moving on:

Remove all traces of the ex from your habitat— including corny first-date memorabilia, Valentine's Day cards (commercialistic crap), all engagement and marriage photos, and barf-worthy sentimental gifts.

Beck's mouth quirked at crap and barf. A woman after his own heart.

Smells are powerful reminders. If after several wash cycles his or her stink remains, burn the item involved.

Stink? Beck eased into a smile.

Music is an excellent purging tool. Download the following and crank to full volume:

"You Oughta Know" by Alanis Morrisette
"Survivor" by Destiny's Child
"Harden My Heart" by Quarterflash

"I'm Free" by Rolling Stones

"Goodbye Earl" by Dixie Chicks

Stock up on beverages. Whether hot chocolate or Appletini's are your poison, make sure you have plenty. You'll need it for step 5.

Throw the party of the year. Invite your closest friends and whoop it up. Thank them for supporting you. Forget the past. Move forward.

Let Divorce Diva Daily help you help yourself.

Okay, so the ending lacked the chutzpah of the earlier tips, but he kinda liked this diva. Sure, she was touting a spiel for business, but he could see the appeal in forgetting the past and moving forward.

He'd done a stand-up job of that himself. It was what drove him every day. Making sure he earned enough money and held enough power to ensure he'd never again have to tolerate the condescending, pitiful stares of people looking down on him because he had nothing.

Growing up destitute in Checkerville ensured he'd bottled those feelings of resentment and bitterness. He had used them to great effect studying endlessly to win a scholarship to college, cramming all-nighters to ace tests, and scrimping every cent he earned in part-time jobs to buy land in Vegas just before the boom hit.

Yeah, he'd shown them all. But it was days like today, when the investors stared at him with the same condescension he'd experienced in his youth that old insecurities he thought long buried flared to life. Everyone in Vegas had a past and he'd paid his dues: self-made millionaire who'd grown up tough. He hadn't hidden his past from anyone, which made their rejection now all the more infuriating.

Annoyed at the turn his thoughts were taking, he hit the "About Us" button and scanned for the price list— nada but

"Price on Application." He didn't trust POA. Price on Application gave potential shysters free rein. The last thing Lou needed now was to be shafted by a shady online company.

He checked the contact details, coming up with an email address to a faceless provider. No phone number. No address. Definitely shady.

Like that'd stop him. With a few clicks of his mouse, he'd messaged a PI who'd done some work for him when hiring prospective employees. Beck didn't like surprises and he didn't trust an anonymous website.

In less than five minutes he had more information. Links between the quirky divorce diva and a party planning company in Provost that had candid testimonials from an extensive list of genuine clientele.

Which made him wonder. Why wouldn't the diva capitalize on the positive PR of an established company? What did she have to hide?

Instincts told him to blow off this diva and find a legit planner, but what if Lou balked and wasted more time? Beck needed a new plan to wow the investors, and that meant having Lou back on board ASAP.

The fastest option would be to follow through with Lou's choice and get this party happening. To do that, he'd have a face-to-face meeting with the diva by the end of the day.

Then he'd focus on more important matters: like finding a quickie wife.

"SLEAZY."

"You think?" Poppy Collins stopped scrolling through

her playlists for appropriate break-up songs to add to her new blog and glared at her BFF, Ashlee.

"Divorce is painful for a lot of people. And you're making fun of it." Ashlee pointed at the computer screen where Poppy had uploaded her latest post for Divorce Diva Daily, the blog that would single-handedly save Party Hard, her sister's party planning business.

"I'm intending on making a lot of money from it," Poppy muttered, tossing her cell on the desk and swinging her chair to face Ashlee. "Money that's going to keep you employed."

Ashlee winced. "Financials that bad?"

"You're Sara's assistant. You tell me." Poppy hated seeing her driven, career-oriented sister in a deep depression that had almost cost her the business. She hated seeing Sara's smug, WASP ex Wayne, prancing around town in a midlife-crisis-red convertible more.

Suburban Provost on the outskirts of Los Angeles wasn't big enough for both of them, which was why Poppy had insisted that Sara recuperate at a private clinic in LA while Poppy put her freelance promotion business on hold, utilized her marketing degree, and ran the business.

Problem was, Poppy knew as much about party planning as she did about relationships: absolutely zilch.

The divorce party idea was her last stand. It had to work. Sara had lost Wayne the Pain. No way would Poppy let her lose her prized business, too. It was all Sara had left.

"But celebrating divorce is tacky," Ashlee said, her gaze drawn to the PC screen again. "We'll get crucified by every do-gooder along the western seaboard."

"That's why Divorce Diva is anonymous. Plus Sara would throw a hissy fit over the D-word, so best to keep this under the radar." Poppy tapped her temple. "Up here for thinking." She pointed at her favorite crimson pumps with the three-inch stiletto heels covered in sparkles. "Down there for dancing."

"Planning parties online is one thing. What if someone wants a one-on-one consult?" Ashlee's frown deepened.

"You're not a party planner. You're a party pooper." Poppy blew out a long breath. "One step at a time, okay?"

"I've got a bad feeling about this."

"And I've got a worse one about this." Poppy stabbed at the stack of bills teetering next to her in-tray. "This idea doesn't take off? We're history."

And Sara would lose everything. No way would she let that happen. She owed her sister. Big time.

Ashlee made disapproving clicking noises. "But divorce is so...so..."

"Inevitable? Guaranteed? Worth celebrating?"

"Private. Painful. Devastating."

"And that's exactly why I'm doing this."

Poppy had seen what impending divorce had done to Sara. Her vibrant, career-driven sis had fallen apart when Wayne walked out, and she'd been a zombie for months, popping anti-depressants until Poppy organized a prolonged stay at the clinic, complete with on-site psychologists. Sara had made progress, but to see her listless without an ounce of spark rammed home for Poppy the fact that love came with risks. Big ones.

Despite the best medical supervision, counseling, and medication, Sara languished, rehashing every reason why her marriage had failed. Poppy could've saved her a fortune in therapy bills with the truth: Wayne was an immature asshole who'd spend his life and fortune searching for the next best thing. Guys like him were never happy with what they had for long. They grew bored. They needed shiny new toys. They kept looking for something bigger and better. Splashing their cash around, seeking vicarious thrills...but they were never truly happy. Narcissistic jerks.

When Sara was ready, Poppy would help her move on with the biggest damned divorce party she could throw. Until then, it was imperative she kept Divorce Diva a secret from her stressed-out sis. With Sara's divorce imminent, no way would she approve, and Poppy didn't want her idea scuttled before it had a chance to work. Or worse, cause a relapse when Sara had finally begun to make progress.

Poppy would do whatever it took to save Sara's business. Plenty of time later to clue Sara in—after she'd succeeded.

"Divorce parties are all about marking the end of suffering and starting fresh. We have rituals for everything else—weddings, births, deaths—why not divorce?"

Ashlee said nothing, her compressed lips and dent between her brows conveying her disapproval.

"A new phase in life is worth celebrating." Damned straight she'd help Sara celebrate The Pain's exit. But if Ashlee didn't buy the professional spiel Poppy had concocted, prospective clients wouldn't either and that would signal the end. "Plus it can be an opportunity for the newly single to thank all the people who've stood by him or her during the ordeal."

Another thing that had torn Sara apart was losing so many of her friends, those tiresome couples who were happy to hang out with other married peeps but scattered when the couple split. What was up with that? Like friendships were expendable or based on the glittery bauble on your ring finger?

"Friends can throw a party to show their divorcing pal they're supported and not alone. Or it can be a time to vent, cry, yell, laugh, whatever, in the company of people who love you." Sara had done enough crying. Poppy would ensure she whooped it up at her divorce party. "What's so bad about that?"

"I still say it's tacky." Starry-eyed, recently engaged Ashlee would think anything tarnishing the holy sanctity of marriage was tacky. Wait until dearly beloved Craig started working nights and taking longer interstate trips and deleting text messages as soon as they pinged. Then she'd get a reality check.

"We're not promoting divorce. We're giving people the option to celebrate it once it's final." Poppy pushed a stack of literature across the desk toward Ashlee. "I've researched this thoroughly. Divorce parties are the latest and greatest. Party planners are raking it in. We have to do this, it's good business."

"I guess." Ashlee gnawed her bottom lip and darted a nervous glance at the stack of bills.

"No guesswork. Divorce Diva Daily is going to rock." Feigning confidence, Poppy interlocked her hands behind her head and leaned back.

"It better. Or we'll be back serving ice creams at Iggy's." Ashlee made a mock gagging motion and Poppy wrinkled her nose at memories of their first job in high school. Iggy had a thing for cones—of every variety—and often rocked up to the shop stoned out of his head, sharing the love by feeling up his employees and giving away freebies. The only reason he was still in business was customer loyalty. Provost looked after its own. Poppy hoped that kind of loyalty extended to Party Hard if her Divorce Diva Daily idea went belly-up and Sara lost everything.

"It'll work, trust me."

Ashlee perched on the desk. "Like how I trusted you with my mom's bachelorette party and we almost landed in jail?" She held up her fingers and started counting off misdemeanors. "Like how I trusted you with my secret make-out place and the entire tenth grade ended up there? Like—"

"Build a bridge, hon." Poppy grinned and waved away Ashlee's concerns, thankful her best friend was along for a ride that promised to be bumpy at best.

A smile tugged at the corners of Ashlee's mouth. "I'll get over it when you prove you've matured beyond high school."

"Hey, I'm mature."

Ashlee raised an imperious eyebrow and pointed at her desk. "You're saving a printed RPatz autographed Twilight flyer, your Gryffindor Forever stick-on tattoos are plastered everywhere, and you've been clubbing three times this week."

"I like to bust a move."

"And the rest?"

"Can never have enough sparkly vamps or Harry Potter around."

"Just make this work, okay?" Ashlee's reluctant smile turned into a full-fledged grin as she tapped the stack of bills with a magenta-tipped fingernail.

"You bet." Poppy saluted. It wasn't until Ashlee bustled out of her office that Poppy slumped in her seat, glaring at the bills like they were radioactive.

No matter how many times Divorce Diva Daily recommended songs like Stevie Nicks's "Stop Dragging Your Heart Around" or ELO's "Don't Bring Me Down," they needed parties to plan.

First request that came in? She'd bust her ass making it the best damned divorce party ever.

No problemo.

TWO

Divorce Diva Daily recommends:
Playlist: "Kissing a Fool" by Michael Bublé
Movie: 10 Things I Hate About You
Cocktail: Rusty Nail

"We have a major problemo." Poppy read the email for the tenth time, wondering if she needed glasses.

She could've sworn some Vegas hotshot had demanded her presence in his office at eight p.m. today. With the promise of an impressive five-figure sum if she threw the divorce party of the year.

Like hell. She'd grown up surrounded by rich pricks who expected everyone around them to dance to the "Money, Money, Money" tune. Lucky for her, she'd quit listening to Abba a long time ago.

Having über-rich parents who were plastic surgeons to the stars had been cool when she'd wanted a pony and a jumping castle, but the gloss had worn off as she grew older, surrounded by fake schmoozing, air-kisses, and selfishness. Their complete disregard for Sara's situation, with minimal financial and emotional aid? Not surprising. If it didn't benefit them, they weren't interested.

She couldn't stand the phoneys who assumed money bought class. Wayne, Sara's ex, had been a classic example: flinging his cash around to impress her sister, reeling her in, then tiring of her and moving on to the next plaything.

While Poppy hated seeing Sara so devastated, a small part of her had secretly been glad when the jerk left. Sara could do so much better than The Pain.

Thoughts of Sara brought her back to the email and Mr. Megabucks' arrogant summons.

Poppy yearned to tell him where he could stick his cash, but that kind of money would go a long way to saving Sara's ailing business. And a mega cash injection from a bigwig could launch Divorce Diva.

But was this guy for real? Eight today? On his private jet? With twenty-grand on the table?

Damn, he was seriously testing her vow to stay anonymous to protect Sara from anything remotely associated with divorce.

"What's the problem?" Ashlee squinted at the email over her shoulder. "Sounds perfectly legit to me." She rolled her eyes. "If you believe in the Tooth Fairy."

"Gave up on fairy tales a long time ago, Ash, which is why this sounds fishy. Not to mention the anonymity factor to protect Sara." She jabbed at the computer screen. "Email only? No one-on-one consultations? Any of this ringing a bell?"

"Told you this diva business would come back to bite you on the butt." Ashlee smirked.

"Yeah, that's you, a regular glass-half-full kinda gal."

Ashlee ignored her sarcasm as Poppy's gaze returned to that twenty grand. Maybe she could make an exception this one time and get Mr. Megabucks to sign a confidentiality agreement to keep her identity secret? That way she'd score the cash and protect Sara. Bonus.

"Did you look him up?"

"Just about to." Poppy typed "Beck Blackwood" into the search engine and almost flipped when an image of the guy popped up on her screen.

"Holy hotties," Ashlee muttered, shouldering her aside to take a closer look. "You're getting on that plane, right?"

"It's a jet," Poppy said, amazed she managed to string three words together without drooling all over her keyboard.

"Jet, schmet, you're going."

The longer Poppy stared at the Gerard Butler–lookalike, the harder it was to come up with a valid reason why she shouldn't.

Unruly caramel curls. Cut-glass jaw. Intense green eyes. Rugged and raw and potent. Holy hottie, indeed.

"It's twenty big ones. You can't not go."

Good point. But the longer Poppy stared at Beck Blackwood's picture, the harder it was to ignore the squirm of butterflies unfolding their wings and getting ready to hold a rave in her belly.

"I hate when hotshots snap their fingers and expect everyone around them to jump."

Ashlee snorted. "For him, I'd jump to the moon and back if he asked."

"Shouldn't you be blinded to hot guys? Engaged bliss and all that crap?" Poppy smiled and pointed at Ashlee's glittering one-and-a-half carat pear-shaped yellow diamond.

"I'm engaged, not dead." Ashlee hid her hand behind her back and pointed at the screen with her other. "And that guy's hot enough to make any woman forget her name, let alone impending marital status."

Poppy had to agree. Didn't mean it changed a thing. She needed to maintain anonymity for Sara's sake, and despite the substantial cash temptation, she had to decline.

The phone rang and Ashlee darted off to answer it, leaving Poppy to compose a polite refusal.

Dear Mr. Blackwood, Thanks for your offer but I'm unable to accept at this time.

All the best with your party planning endeavors.

The team at Divorce Diva Daily.

Poppy fired off the email, satisfied with the perfect combination of courteous and gracious. Establishing distance with the sign-off had been a stroke of genius, too. How could he get uptight against an entire "team"?

About to file away his email and give in to a hankering for a double-shot caramel latte at the café next door, her hand hovered over the mouse to shut down her inbox when a response pinged.

Surprised—she hadn't expected to hear from him again at all, let alone so fast—she opened the email. And nearly fell off her chair.

Dear Diva, Our meeting tonight is an order, not a request.

I assume you have good reason to maintain your anonymity, so if you value your association with Party Hard I'll expect your arrival at 8 p.m. Sharp.

Beck Blackwood.

She read the email twice to make sure she wasn't hallucinating.

"Son of a bitch," she muttered, knuckling her eyes before refocusing and reading a third time. The jerk was blackmailing her. Worse, he knew about Party Hard.

Freaking hell. She reined in her first urge to fire back a short, sharp retort—along the lines of "eff-off"—and tried to think this through. If he hadn't pissed her off enough with his high and mighty summons before, his arrogant response to her refusal would've done it.

Who the hell did he think he was, giving her an order? Someone needed to tell him the King of Vegas had died a long time ago.

And he was a smartass, too, deliberately calling her a "diva," implying her behavior was such.

Well, she'd give him diva behavior. In person. Not because she acquiesced to blackmail, but for the simple reason she wanted to see the rich jerk's face when she told him where he could stick his offer.

Her gaze landed on the stack of unpaid bills stuffed into a fuchsia folder and her heart sank.

Who was she kidding? She couldn't afford to knock back twenty grand, not when Party Hard—and Sara— teetered on the brink. And now her number one reason for not meeting him face to face, to protect Sara's anonymity and any association with Divorce Diva Daily, had just evaporated.

Typical. When it came to money, guys like him wouldn't pay up until they knew whom they were dealing with, so it stood to reason he'd probably flung some cash around to investigate her.

The problem was, how much did he know? And could she get him to keep his big mouth shut?

Her pride may have demanded she tell Blackwood to shove it, but her loyalty to Sara insisted she had better make this the pitch of her life.

Damn him. Once she'd sent her terse reply—*See you at eight, Poppy Collins*—she kicked the trashcan. Hard.

Ashlee stuck her head around the doorway. "Everything okay?"

"Fine," Poppy said, glaring at Blackwood's pic that popped up on her screen when she closed her inbox. Bad move. She should've shut down the search engine first, as Ashlee wolf-whistled when she sauntered over to the desk.

"Better than fine, getting up close and personal with 'The Hottie.' " Ashlee made puckering noises and Poppy swatted her away.

She didn't want to explain the online altercation with Blackwood or his attempt at blackmail. Ash would worry, so Poppy decided to play the casual game. She'd handle Beck Blackwood herself.

"I'm pretty sure I won't be getting that close to potentially our biggest—and only—client at this stage, but in case I do, I'll let you know how his technique rates."

"That's my girl." Ashlee slugged her on the arm. "You know you'll be staying overnight in Vegas, right?"

"Hadn't planned to."

"Guys like that will have a hotel room ready and waiting for you." Ashlee spoke slowly, as if Poppy had suddenly developed obtuseness. "He's sending a private jet. What's one little hotel room for the night?"

Now that she'd decided to go, Poppy hadn't counted on a layover, but considering it'd be late when she finished her pitch, maybe she should pack for an overnighter just in case.

"Silk."

"What?"

"Bet The Hottie favors silk lingerie." Ashlee tapped her bottom lip, pondering. "Maybe lace?"

Annoyed by the thought of wearing anything remotely sexy near Beck Blackwood, Poppy waved Ashlee away. "Haven't you got work to do?"

"Yeah, but bet it's not half as fun as your work tonight." Ashlee blew her a kiss as she headed for the door. "And here's another tip. When in Vegas, always bet on black."

"I'm not gambling—"

"Black silk, satin, lace, whatever. LBD, push-up bra, stockings, you'll have him throwing the big bucks at you."

"Dressed like that, it won't be for my party planning skills," Poppy muttered, earning a grin from Ashlee.

"Good luck, hon." Ashlee gave her a thumbs-up sign before heading back to her desk in the outer office.

Poppy didn't need luck. She'd prove to moneybags Blackwood she could match it with the big boys in Vegas and throw a party the city would never forget. Failure wasn't an option.

As for the laid-back, rugged, gorgeous thing he had going on? She'd wear her white cotton, purple polka-dot granny panties to the meeting. It paid to not tempt fate, and considering the dry spell she'd had for the last eight months while juggling Sara's depression and business, she wouldn't want her panties getting any ideas and sliding off at the first sight of those penetrating green eyes.

Yeah, she'd head to this meeting in Vegas well prepared. Beck Blackwood wouldn't know what hit him.

"MAKE MINE A DOUBLE."

"You've had enough." Beck shook his head and slid the aged whiskey out of Lou's reach. "Time to call it a night."

"You're no fun." Lou glared at him through slightly glazed eyes, spoiling his mean look by semi-sliding off the stool. "I know why, too. It's because those investors screwed us this morning."

Beck reassessed. Lou couldn't be completely hammered if he was astute enough to home in on the one reason behind Beck's foul mood. But the last thing Beck felt like doing was rehashing this morning. Not while bitterness still burned his gut.

"Wanna know what I think?" Lou slammed a hand on the table, making the whiskey glasses clink. "Screw the investors. And screw Julie, the money-hungry, soul-sucking, bee-yatch—"

"Come on, big boy, time for bed." Beck had to interject before Lou launched on another abusive tirade. He'd never liked Lou's ex, but Julie didn't deserve the crap Lou was heaping on her. They'd both screwed up and divorce had been inevitable. Beck could've told him so at the start and saved them both the angst and a small fortune slugging it out via lawyers.

Marriage was the pits. And then you divorced. Simple equation. Which was why he avoided doing the math.

Beck slid a hand under Lou's elbow to help him up, but his friend shrugged him off with surprising force.

"Screw you. I wanna party."

Dragging in a deep breath, Beck mentally counted to ten. He didn't have time for this. He had to meet with the party planner at eight, and considering it was now seven, he was done babysitting. "I'm meeting with your planner soon, so save your partying for next weekend."

"Been a long time since I partied hard." Lou slumped lower in his chair. "A ball and chain does that to a guy. Next weekend...yeah, sounds good..." Lou's gaze focused on the muted TV over Beck's shoulder, eyes narrowed as he leaned forward. "Turn that up."

Beck glanced at his watch, groaned, and stabbed at the volume button on the remote in time to catch the end of a segment on divorce parties from a well-respected current-affairs show.

"See? Told you throwing a party to celebrate my freedom is cool." Lou leaped from his chair, staggered a little, before gaining his balance. "I'm a frigging genius."

Debatable, as Beck took in Lou's crumpled shirt, unkempt trousers, and rumpled jacket.

But the faster he appeased his friend, the faster he'd get him off to bed so he could meet the planner and tick one more thing off his extensive to-do list.

"I'll hash out the details tonight and fill you in tomorrow."

"Maybe I should come with you? Help plan?" Lou peered at him through bleary eyes and Beck knew if the party planner took one look at him she'd re-board the jet for LA. "I can help. Divorce parties are hip, all the celebs are doing it. Even the local business journal said so."

Beck couldn't give a shit whether the governor himself approved of divorce parties. He needed to appease Lou so he could get this thing done and move onto more important matters, like planning his next line of attack with the investors. And finding himself a wife.

"So you checked out that website link I gave you?" Before Beck could bundle him toward the nearest elevator, Lou had whipped out his smartphone and brought up Divorce Diva Daily, grinning inanely as he peered at the website. "Yep, I'm going to get me a little divorce diva to throw the biggest damned party Vegas has ever seen."

"Got it. Big party. I'll tell her."

"I'll come meet her—"

"No."

Lou finally picked up on the *Don't jerk me around* intonation, and nodded. "Okay. But this party has to be mega."

He threw his arms wide. "I want the whole goddamn town to know nobody gets to stick it to Lou Robinson."

"Leave it to me—"

"I need closure." Lou gripped Beck's arm in a surprisingly strong grasp for a near-teetotaler who'd downed three quarters of a bottle of whiskey. "You'll take care of this, right?"

Casting a dubious glance at the website, Beck nodded.

"You know what you need?" Lou jabbed a finger at the website. "The opposite of this."

Beck had to drag Lou to the elevator. Fast.

"You need a wife." Lou grinned like he'd single-handedly solved the world's climate crisis. "Those investors think Blackwood Enterprises is trash? Show them you're not."

The fact his inebriated friend had inadvertently echoed his irrational thoughts from earlier didn't help Beck's mood. "Yeah, maybe I should ask this divorce party chick for marital advice or a fix-up."

"Can't be any worse than this morning." Lou winced. "Smug bastards. Hate uptight pricks like that."

Beck couldn't agree more.

"Maybe the divorce diva runs a dating site, too?" Lou snapped his fingers. "Instant wifey."

"You're insane." Besides, Beck had already thoroughly researched the diva and she didn't moonlight as a matchmaker. Her terse reply to his email summons had made him laugh. What did she think, that he'd go into a face-to-face consult unprepared? Would be interesting what she came up with when he confronted her. Would she scuttle him with BS or tell the truth?

"Drunk and insane," Beck amended.

"You have to admit, the chick has style." Lou chuckled as he scanned the diva's website and Beck couldn't help but take a look. The fact that she'd made him laugh with her first blog entry? A one-off.

BURN BABY BURN

The physical fallout from a marriage break-up can be the pits. Reminders of your ex everywhere you turn, from old razors lurking in bathroom cabinets to slash unsuspecting fingers, to ratty T-shirts with obnoxious slogans you once tolerated all in the name of love (barf!).

He snickered.

Divorce Diva Daily's advice today is "Burn, baby, burn." A burning ceremony can be cathartic. You may like to burn:

Your marriage certificate

A list of things you won't miss (e.g., remote control hogging, snoring, neuroses á la "Do I look fat in this?", makeup remnants from the sixties, etc.)

Photos

A replica of the ex's privates

All of the above

A burning ritual signifies letting go, a proactive way to move on. And if you can't burn, flushing or shredding works just as effectively.

Beck found himself grinning inanely and Lou sniggered. She'd done it again. Made him laugh. Something he didn't do much of these days.

It made him all the more curious about the woman who'd answered his email. He had no idea if Poppy Collins was the divorce diva or an underling, but considering she'd be in his office in an hour, he'd soon find out. Everyone had a weak spot.

He'd learned that the hard way. It was why he abhorred weakness of any kind, why he'd developed a hard outer shell by the time he hit preschool. Being raised by Pa had toughened him, but he had his absentee parents to thank for teaching him the art of indifference from an early age.

Before they shot up and killed themselves, that is.

"If she's this cool in real life, my party's going to rock." Lou swiped his finger across the smartphone, squinting his eyes to read the fine print. "Did you see the links to high-profile business mags and journals? Even Los Angeles Business Weekly reported divorce parties are the latest, greatest thing."

"Saw that. Also saw the part where it said divorce party planners are doing brisk business and raking in healthy profits."

"You're a cynic." Lou glanced up, the hint of vulnerability in his blurry eyes making Beck feel like a bastard.

Lou was going through a rough time. The least he could do was be supportive.

Who knew misery paid? These parties may be about consoling and support and celebrating a new life phase, but to Beck, they reeked of sadness and bitterness and anger. Then again, Lou had been moping around, his mind not one hundred percent focused on work, so if this dumb divorce party purged his blues, Beck was all for it.

"Pays to be cautious, my friend."

"Bet you researched this diva." Lou snorted. "You vet everybody."

"I checked into her." And found nothing telling. A private Facebook page Beck couldn't access, a few articles she'd written for a high school newspaper in suburban Provost, no pictures. Damn.

After the PI had given him the link between Divorce Diva Daily and a respectable party planning company in Provost, he'd wanted more on the would-be charlatan. He'd come up with nothing. Her initial refusal to meet surprised him. Money talked, and he'd expected the twenty grand he'd dangled as incentive to meet him would serve its purpose.

Interesting. For someone hiding behind a computer screen, his jab at revealing her links to Party Hard had been more of an enticement to meet than the money.

Why? What did the divorce diva have to hide? And did it involve screwing over her customers? Too bad for her the one thing he enjoyed as much as accumulating a fortune was solving mysteries.

And she'd just moved to the top of his to-do list. "Come on, big fella, time to get you to bed so I can go organize this rocking party."

"You're the best," Lou mumbled, shrugging off Beck's attempt at help and staggering toward the elevator.

Not yet, he wasn't, but Beck intended on being the best. When he secured the nationwide deal, he'd prove it.

THREE

Divorce Diva Daily recommends:
Playlist: "You Give Love a Bad Name" by Bon Jovi
Movie: Something's Gotta Give
Cocktail: Fallen Angel

As the jet touched down in Vegas, Poppy wriggled in her seat, craning for a better view.

She loved this town. Loved the glitz and glamor, the razzle-dazzle, the surrealism of not sleeping if you didn't want to. She'd visited twice, once with Ashlee after they'd graduated high school and another time with a guy she'd been seeing for a month.

The first time she'd shopped and done the shows circuit and partied her way through the three days with Ashlee. The second time, she drank her way through the weekend when the guy turned out to be a gambling fiend who had ditched her to play blackjack.

This visit promised to be very different. As the jet

taxied along the runway, she glanced at her surroundings, impressed despite her snit with its owner.

Butter-soft leather recliners the color of ripe wheat lined one side of the jet, directly opposite a mahogany bar with forest green leather bar stools edging it. The flat-screen TV above the bar was larger than her bedroom back home. Squishy ochre cushions placed strategically on the chairs highlighted their pristine lushness, while the mahogany coffee tables were so highly polished she could have used them as mirrors.

The opulent luxury made her feel like she'd stumbled into a princess' dream. And that was before she'd been personally served a late lunch of sesame-crusted tempura shrimp served with a watercress and pear salad, rose-stewed figs and baklava, and hand-squeezed lemonade by a steward. She would've preferred to take him up on his offer of Moët, but she needed her faculties clear and functioning for her meeting with Beck Blackwood. For all she knew, it might be a ploy to get her tipsy so he could take advantage of her. A girl could dream, right?

As the jet's only other occupant, the steward had been attentive yet deferent, and Poppy had almost wished Beck Blackwood had summoned her to Miami.

She could get used to this. Her parents were loaded, but they weren't rich enough for private jets. First class had been a bonus. She despised the moneyed social circles she'd been raised in, but when it came to flying? Tattoo a giant "H" on her forehead for "hypocrite."

"Traffic is backed up on the ground, Miss Collins, so you'll be disembarking in ten minutes."

"Thanks." She smiled at the steward, who tipped his cap before easing behind the door at the rear of the plane.

Ten minutes gave her time to do a quick blog update before prepping the pitch of her life.

She'd just fired up her tablet when the phone on the bar rang.

She ignored it, until the steward stuck his head around the back partition. "That'll be for you, Miss Collins."

"Who—" But he'd already vanished and with a sinking feeling, she headed for the phone. Only one person would be calling her on a private jet. *His* private jet.

Great. The plane had barely touched down and Mr. Megabucks was already expecting her to jump to his tune. Billionaires and their blasted foibles.

She answered the phone. "Poppy Collins speaking."

A long pause made the hairs on the nape of her neck snap to attention.

"Hope you're quicker off the mark with your pitch than you are answering phones."

Hot damn. She knew he had the look, and now she knew he had the voice to go with it. Deep. Resonant. Commanding. With an edge of huskiness that suggested all-night sex with no regrets.

A host of smartass retorts sprung to Poppy's lips, but she clamped the urge to use them. If Beck Blackwood was serious about the offer of twenty big ones, she couldn't afford to piss him off. Time enough for that later, after he'd signed on the dotted line.

"I was busy going over my presentation." She injected the right amount of subservience to appease the arrogant puppet-master. "What can I do for you?"

"Sure you want me to answer that?"

Was he flirting with her? Maybe she should've fortified those granny panties. With steel.

"We're meeting shortly, Mr. Blackwood. Unless there's

a point to this phone call, I'd like to get back to my presentation."

He snickered. "Snark. Like your blog."

"You read it?"

She mentally slapped herself upside the head. Of course he would've read it. If his investigators had discovered her link to Party Hard, they probably knew everything from her preferred cereal to her cup size.

"It's entertaining in its own way." Way to go with the backhanded compliment. She should let it go. But she'd had enough of his condescension, mega payoff or not.

"In its own way?"

"For a fluff piece."

She heard the hint of amusement and it was the only thing that prevented her from telling him where he could stick his divorce party. That and the memory of the last time she'd seen Sara: pale, listless, morose, and overmedicated.

"Did my reference to your fluff piece offend you?"

He was baiting her. He wanted her to bite back. Let him wait.

"Lucky for me that fluff grabbed your attention long enough for you to fly me out here to plan a party you'll never forget."

This time he laughed out loud. "I like confidence in a woman."

"Then you'll love me." She winced, instantly regretting her sassy comeback. She didn't want any guy to love her, not in any sense. Love was for losers. Masochistic losers.

Though she shouldn't knock it, considering those losers would keep Party Hard afloat, courtesy of her Divorce Diva Daily ingenuity.

"We'll see," he said, the uncomfortable edge underlying

his tone matching her squirm-factor at the remotest mention of the L-word. "See you soon."

Before she could respond, he hung up, leaving her perplexed as she stared at the phone. What the hell was that all about? She had no idea why he'd called, and second-guessing his motivation didn't help her burgeoning nerves.

For despite a foolproof presentation designed to wow, she was nervous.

This had to work. For all their sakes.

Poppy smoothed her skirt and tugged at the hem of her jacket as she stepped onto the tarmac. She'd gone for understated elegance: pinstriped ebony suit with a below-knee pencil skirt, three-inch patent heels, and stockings. Her only concession to her usual flair was a crimson silk shirt that elevated the suit from prim to possibilities.

She wanted to wow Beck Blackwood. To show him she wasn't some underling who jumped when he snapped his fingers and flung his cash around, even though that was exactly what she'd done.

She squared her shoulders, tucked her satchel under her arm, and marched toward the limousine waiting nearby. In a town where limos were the norm rather than the exception, this one stood out: long, silver, shapely.

After the jet, it figured. Beck Blackwood had the best of everything and wouldn't settle for anything less. Lucky for him, she intended on being the best in the party planning business.

As she neared the limo, the back passenger door opened and a hint of premonition strummed her spine. The limo had a passenger, and with the chauffeur waiting a few discreet feet away, that passenger had to be important enough to command privacy.

Her step faltered as Beck Blackwood stepped from the

limo, imposing and arresting and way too gorgeous to be legal.

Hell. When he said *See you soon* she'd assumed he'd meant his office. She hadn't expected a welcoming committee, though by his shuttered expression he was none too welcoming.

He watched her approach and her skin prickled with every step. There was nothing overtly sexual in his steady stare, but every nerve ending in her body went on high alert the closer she got.

Ashlee had labeled him a hottie. He was so far beyond hottie in the flesh it wasn't funny.

When she'd envisioned their first meeting, it had been in an office with neutral furniture and high-tech gadgets. She'd mentally rehearsed a hundred professional greetings for when an über secretary ushered her into that office.

Sadly, her carefully constructed vocab designed to impress deserted her the moment she got within three feet of the guy.

That pic online, the one bearing a strong resemblance to Gerard Butler? Did. Not. Do. Him. Justice.

Embarrassingly speechless, she did the only thing she could: when in doubt, smile. It must've lost something in the translation and come out an inane grin, because his eyebrow inverted in a comical WTF.

"Nice blouse."

She raised him a WTF eyebrow in return. Of all the introductions she'd imagined, that hadn't been one of them, a strangely intimate comment on her attire.

He was trying to disarm her. It was working. Not that she'd let him know. "Nice tie."

To her surprise he laughed. "Touché."

"Was the color a deliberate choice?" She often wore a

touch of deep crimson—poppy—as a good-luck token, hence her shirt.

He slid a finger beneath the tie's knot, loosening it a tad. It didn't detract from his smooth shark aura. He'd probably gone for a shot-silk poppy tie to goad her. "Poppy seems to be a popular color these days."

She didn't want to ask how he knew that. He probably had a slew of glam girlfriends in slinky, revealing, poppy dresses for every day of the week. The good thing about their absurd color conversation: it gave her time to gather her wits. Time to get this meeting off to a better start.

"Now that we've analyzed this year's most sought-after palette for Fashion Week, should we get down to business?" She held out her hand. "Poppy Collins. Pleased to meet you."

"Beck Blackwood. Likewise." The moment his large hand enveloped hers, she stiffened against the unexpected zap that sizzled up her arm and centered on places it had no right centering.

If she didn't know better, she could've sworn the zap worked both ways, as his pupils widened perceptibly and he quickly released her.

"Call me Beck."

She inclined her head. "Call me stupid."

His eyes widened in surprise and she mentally clapped a hand over her mouth. Too late.

"For agreeing to meet you despite your less than subtle attempt at blackmail?"

His sinful mouth eased into a smirk. One she'd like to wipe off. "Don't take it personally. I vet all the people I hire." The smirk gave way to a practiced smile. "Pays to be alert in any business, as I'm sure you'd appreciate."

Great. Was he saying she was an astute businesswoman,

or warning her to be on her guard? Whatever. She'd come this far, no point alienating him. This party would launch Divorce Diva Daily, and if Hotshot could keep his mouth shut about her identity, this could prove a win-win all around.

"Just so you know, I'm flexible professionally but I don't take orders kindly."

"Noted." That damned smile widened. "Have to say, you're not what I expected." His all-encompassing stare started at her patent pumps and swept upward, coolly assessing, as she crazily wished it'd linger in those places his handshake had zapped a second ago.

"Let me guess. You were expecting bitter and twisted?"

"Would you settle for wary and cynical?"

Not fair. Not only was the guy gorgeous, he had the intelligence and quick wit to match.

"Not married?" His gaze dipped to her ring finger.

"No way," she said, immediately regretting her instinctive outburst under his intense scrutiny.

He had the penetrating stare down pat and she could easily imagine him facing off a boardroom full of adversaries.

She wasn't so easily intimidated. "No engagements, no significant others, no cramping of style." She waved her left hand in his face to prove it.

"And you've got plenty of that." His stare softened into something she didn't dare label.

She preferred the intimidating stare to the admiration tinged with a hint of heat.

"Let's go. We've got a lot of work to do." He reverted to brusque and abrupt, and she preferred it. The less zapping that occurred around Beck, the better. Even thinking of him on a first-name basis implied an intimacy she didn't like.

"After you." He gestured toward the open limo door, his hand brushing the small of her back in gentle guidance.

Yep, the zap was still there. Disconcerting and disarming. She slid into the limo. The sooner she nailed this pitch, the sooner she could head back to the safety of Provost and the anonymity of Divorce Diva Daily.

This was one diva that had no intention of flaunting anything.

∼

BECK SPRAWLED across the seat opposite Poppy, watching her type furiously on her tablet. No hardship, watching her.

He liked the fact she was ignoring him. It meant he had her rattled.

Join the club. She'd shot down his expectations of a dour, bitter, forty-something, middle-aged divorcée the moment she stepped onto the tarmac and he got his first look at the pocket dynamo.

Because that's what she was, fire and ice wrapped in a delicious, petite package. He hadn't banked on the uncharacteristic, almost visceral reaction and it unnerved him.

He'd expected sour and acrimonious, not sizzling and defiant. And her damned voice: rich, teasing, tempting. Brought to mind visions of smoky nightclubs, smooth bourbon, and sultry nights made for sex.

That's what annoyed him the most. He never mixed business with pleasure, and the fact she made him think of sex had him re-evaluating the wisdom of meeting with her. He should've thrown cash at her online and let her do her worst.

The snark didn't help, either. He liked feisty, a woman

to challenge him. He'd never found one yet. Once they discovered who he was, women tended to accede to his judgment or attempt to sway him with vamp factor. Both plays grew tiresome after a while.

Poppy was neither. She'd confronted him about his email demand and issued a subtle warning she wouldn't put up with it again. He admired her bluntness. It bode well for getting this party happening ASAP.

She was definitely the diva behind the website—it didn't take long for her natural impudence to surface in person. And it was a better aphrodisiac than any near-naked showgirl. Or naked one, for that matter.

The instant she'd started matching wits with him, he'd been turned on. Go figure.

He preferred his business dealings to be hard-on free and the fact she'd crept under his guard rankled. He didn't have time for distractions.

"Problem?" She pinned him with a narrow-eyed glare.

"No."

Discounting the one where he couldn't take his eyes off her. He'd bet his last dollar that crimson silk shirt with a hint of cleavage was the real her, bold and flamboyant, and she'd been unable to resist hiding her true self behind a business suit designed to impress.

He was impressed, all right, but it had more to do with the whole package than her suit. Not strictly beautiful, but she had an inherent fire that made her caramel eyes glow with that indefinable something that turned guys' heads.

Heart-shaped face, pert nose, slightly wider than average mouth—he wouldn't go there—shoulder-length layered just-out-of-bed brown hair equaled a striking combination, and that was on top of her enticing curves.

So he was attracted to her. Big deal. Didn't mean he'd act on it.

"Didn't your mother ever tell you it's rude to stare?"

And just like that, his hard-on deflated. "Before or after she overdosed on coke?"

Stricken, she paled and he silently cursed. "Sorry."

"Don't be, I'm not."

He'd given up mourning his parents—or lack of—a long time ago. Wasted energy. His folks had never given a damn about him, had indulged in the selfish lifestyle of druggies who didn't care about anything except their next hit, neglecting their kid in the process.

He'd attended their funerals out of obligation and respect for Pa, who'd been as stoic as him. The Blackwoods were confirmed realists, what was left of the family. Beck respected straight shooting, and Pa was one of the best at it. To this day, Beck believed he'd got into so many fistfights as a kid just so he could listen to Pa dole out his dry commentary on life as he patched him up.

It'd been too long since he'd visited Pa. He'd rectify that once this deal went through.

He glanced out the window as the limo eased along the Strip, the twinkling lights and streaming crowds a comfort. He preferred desert silence over big-city bedlam, but every time he cruised through this town, he knew he'd made it.

Size mattered in Vegas, and he'd gone all out when he'd made his first millions, gambling on property investments rather than slots, ensuring every single person who'd ever doubted him sat up and took notice. Blackwood Enterprises was renowned for its luxury constructions, and he intended for everyone in America to know it.

He gestured out the window. "Been to Vegas before?"

"Twice." She wrinkled her nose.

"You don't like it?"

"It's okay if you like flashy."

"Don't be fooled by the glitz. If you look beneath the surface, there's more on offer."

She eyeballed him and he didn't know what made him more edgy—her ability to undermine him with a glance or the strange feeling she could see down to his soul. "We're talking about the city, right?" Damn, she was good.

"Of course. Making chitchat."

"I have a feeling you never say anything without an end game in sight."

There she went again, pinning him down with an intuition that left him squirming.

He'd aimed to make her uncomfortable by picking her up from the airport. He didn't appreciate having the tables turned.

Time to have a little fun. "We're almost there." He half expected her to call him on his abrupt change of topic and his gruffness. Instead, she sat there, staring at him, silently appraising.

Yeah, definitely time to regain control. "I hope you packed a change of clothes along with your presentation?" He pointed to her giant satchel.

"Why?" The first flicker of uncertainty had her glancing at the bag with the barest of frowns.

"Because you're staying the night. With me."

FOUR

Divorce Diva Daily recommends:
Playlist: "Go Your Own Way" by Fleetwood Mac
Movie: Sleeping with the Enemy
Cocktail: Top of the Sheets

"Three words for you. No freaking way." As the impulsive rebuttal fell from her lips, Poppy hazarded a guess that a powerful guy like Beck wouldn't get refused very often.

Who wouldn't want to spend the night with the guy? Just look at him. So she did, daring him to retract his inappropriate declaration.

He didn't appear angry. In fact, the corners of his mouth curved in amusement. "I'm not sure what kind of guy you think I am, but I can assure you when I made my offer for you to spend the night, I merely referred to one of the apartments in a hotel I own."

His mouth eased into a full-blown grin, like he'd trumped her.

As if. Royal flush beat full house every time. "You do this often, don't you?"

Confusion clouded his eyes for a second. "Do what?"

"Bait and switch. Bait your opponent, reel them in a little, then switch to disingenuous." She shrugged. "Nice technique, but wasted on me."

"Is that so?" His eyes narrowed but couldn't hide the glint of admiration.

"Yeah, because I don't have time for games. I'm here to show you I'm the best there is in the party planning biz, that's it. Take it or leave it."

Foolish fighting words, when the last thing she could afford was for him to leave it. But she'd figured out pretty damn quick that Beck Blackwood preferred honesty. She was counting on it.

"Are you always this confrontational with your clients?"

No, only the ones who looked like a god and who had the capability to seriously derail her. She didn't like feeling uncertain, hated feeling out of place among her folks' uppity friends as a kid. So she'd developed a backbone early, learning that standing up for herself earned respect and being proactive got results.

Wallflowers came in last, and she'd hated coming last growing up. Rozelle and Earl Collins may have been renowned LA plastic surgeons, but as parents? They sucked.

While her folks put in long hours with the beautiful people who needed their faces, boobs, and butts rearranged, enhanced, and lifted, Sara had raised her. From her homework to her first period, from her first love to graduation, Sara had been there for her when her folks hadn't been. That was why Poppy was here now, taking crap from a supercilious charmer and putting herself on the line to save

Sara's business. She'd do whatever it took for her sis to hang onto the one thing she had left.

She needed Beck Blackwood. Correction: she needed his business. Getting the two mixed up would end in disaster.

"Honesty's important to me. I assumed it would be to a businessman like you, too?"

"Okay then, why don't we start the pitch a little early?" He watched her, thoughtful, as if he couldn't quite figure out what she was up to. "Tell me your credentials."

Uh-oh, this isn't what she wanted. When she pitched her ideas she'd envisioned office space between them, a PowerPoint presentation at her fingertips, and a host of facts to dazzle him. She hadn't imagined being cocooned in the intimacy of a limo, his crisp citrus aftershave blending with the interior's new-leather smell for an intoxicating richness that tantalized her senses.

She hated how uncertain he made her feel—and how good he smelled. "I'd prefer to use visuals to accompany my presentation."

"What, celebratory handcuffs and phallic cakes?"

To her annoyance, heat surged to her cheeks. "Divorce Diva Daily doesn't do tacky."

"Then tell me, what do you do?" He braced his elbows on his knees and leaned forward, immediately shrinking the limo space further.

Damn, she couldn't put him off. She'd have to give him something without compromising the kick-ass presentation she'd fast-tracked earlier today.

"We focus on classy celebrations of freedom. No bitterness, no rehashing the past, no dwelling—our aim is to focus on the future." She held up her hand, fingers extended, ready to tick off points. "Food. Drink. Music. Entertainment. The staples of any great party, but we gear it toward the individual in such a way they have the time of their lives without any regrets. Leave the past behind, celebrate the future, that's basically our motto."

He continued to watch her, coolly assessing. She didn't like the silence, so she plowed on. "As for my credentials, I'm a freelancer. I have a marketing degree and have worked on several major motion picture campaigns in Hollywood."

He raised an eyebrow. "That doesn't sound like party planning experience to me."

Fan-freaking-tastic. She'd hoped to impress him with her real skills. Trust Einstein to home in on what she hadn't said. She could lie, bluff her way out of it, verbally pad her résumé. But she'd told him she was honest and he'd probably seen through her. "My sister owns the business. I help out on occasion, but she's taking a break at the moment, so you get me instead."

She could've sworn she heard him mutter "Lucky me," their locked gazes underlined by a sizzle she'd rather not define.

To her relief, he leaned back and she felt like she could breathe again.

"So you're the diva, huh?"

"Only at work. Away from it, I'm a pussycat."

Where had that come from? Sounded like she was flirting with him. Not good.

"De-clawed, I hope?"

"Where's the fun in that?"

The good news? She'd distracted him from badgering her for the rest of her presentation.

The bad news? They'd somehow moved beyond work into murky territory.

"You're an intriguing woman."

The way he said it, with a hint of admiration, and the way he looked at her, like he couldn't tear his gaze away, made her feel squirmy and proud and desired all at the same time.

So she did what she always did when rattled: deflect with humor. "That's what they all say."

Thankfully, the limo glided to a stop at that moment and effectively ended their conversation.

Good. She couldn't handle much more of being confined with the hotshot, her every move and word being scrutinized. Time to nail this presentation and head back to Provost as fast as his private jet could take her, far from green eyes and quirky smiles and bedroom voices.

∽

BECK HAD NEVER BEEN SO glad to enter the safety of his office. While many of his colleagues considered home to be their sanctuary, this place was his. It was where he did his best thinking, where he could shut out the world, where he could escape from being constantly scrutinized.

He'd hated that as a kid, being stared at, though back then it had been with ridicule and derision. These days he commanded respect and attention through his achievements and he'd worked his ass off to get it, but every now and then he longed for the simplicity of lying beneath the stars, the clearness of the desert sky above, the residual warmth from a scorching day in the sand beneath.

"Nice view." As he stared at Poppy, propped against the floor to ceiling glass window overlooking a glittering Vegas far below, he couldn't agree more. "Sensational."

An inflection in his tone must've alerted her he wasn't talking about the view. She turned slowly, her gaze questioning. Let her wonder. He had no intention of answering, considering he had no idea what it was about the bold woman that had him thinking beyond her pitch and how he could convince her to stay the night with him. For real.

He'd been taunting earlier, interested to see how she'd handle being on the defensive. She'd impressed him with her ability to think quickly, to parry and deflect, and it had added to her appeal. He shouldn't have shown weakness in admitting she intrigued him. Weakness resulted in failure. But there was something about her bluntness that demanded the same.

"Go ahead and set up. I'll check my messages." Anything to distract from the surprising urge to say screw the presentation and take her out for a night on the town she'd never forget.

"Okey-dokey." She fiddled with PowerPoint on her tablet as he checked his emails, one in particular catching his eye.

He scanned the email, the contents making his fingers curl into fists under the desk. Swallowing a string of invective curses, he wished he could clamp Stan's balls in a vice, and return the favor the big guy was doing to him.

According to Stan, another construction company could be tendering for the nationwide hotel deal, so if Blackwood Enterprises wanted to stay in contention, Beck had to get his ass into gear.

Good old Stan used polite terminology but that was the gist of the email. Not only did he need a wife to gain respectability, he needed it done yesterday.

Beck was used to tight deadlines, but this? Tough task.

"I'm ready whenever you are," Poppy said.

And as he glanced at her, all tempting curves and firecracker mouth, the answer to his problems detonated in an explosion of logic and foolhardiness.

Fuck, it was a crazy solution, but with his time frame? He had to go for it.

But he'd ease into it first, mention the idea of needing a wife, see how she reacted. Then he'd let her give her spiel, throw in a mega-cash incentive she couldn't refuse, and lay the rest of his cards on the table. He wouldn't accept anything less than a winning hand.

"I know the diva can plan parties, but how good are you at finding me a wife?"

FIVE

Divorce Diva Daily recommends:
Playlist: "Never Again" by Nickelback
Movie: Must Love Dogs
Cocktail: Pisco Sour

Beck Blackwood may be sex on legs but the guy was totally loco.

"Pardon?"

"Can you help me find a wife?" He stood, managing to look imposing and appealing simultaneously.

Laughter bubbled in her throat but she swallowed it when he frowned.

He was serious. Yep, completely loco. "Sorry, I do parties. Try a dating service."

"I need a wife fast." His frown deepened and the pulse in his neck became noticeable.

"Why? You knocked up?" she deadpanned.

His eyes widened in surprise before he grinned. "Anyone you can recommend?"

"For the position of wife?" She pretended to ponder, tapping a fingernail against her bottom lip. "Let me see. Someone who's crazy enough to marry a guy she doesn't know?" She snapped her fingers. "Nope. Sorry. Plum out of candidates."

"You've got a smart mouth."

"Matches the rest of me." She pointed at her presentation ready to go. "If you'd ever let me show you."

He hesitated, as if he wanted to push the issue, but acquiesced with a slight nod instead. "Go ahead."

The guy wanted a wife, pronto. What was he, some kind of desperado? And why the hell would a guy like him need a wife fast anyway? Determinedly ignoring her rampant curiosity, she waited until he sat on one of the low-slung gunmetal gray leather sofas nearby before firing up the first slide.

"As I mentioned earlier, Divorce Diva Daily is all about class." She hit the button to bring up the next slide. "Humans are ritualistic. We like rituals. They make us feel secure and part of a community. So that's what a divorce party does. It gives the injured party a way to cope with this difficult transition."

He sat there, immovable. It didn't help her nerves. "A new phase in a person's life is beginning and a divorce party is a great way to announce your new status." She made air-quotes with her fingers. "Hey, I'm single and up for new experiences and new relationships."

He didn't blink and her disappointment spiraled. "It's the perfect way to mark the end of pain and suffering and embrace a new life."

Still nothing. She took a deep breath before launching

into the finale. "Basically, whatever works we provide. If voodoo dolls, dart throwing, piñata smashing is the way to go, we'll tailor a party around that. If a classy cocktail party with fab music and amazing food is preferred, we can do that. We're flexible."

She wound up her spiel, seeking some kind of positive feedback: the slightest positive nod, a glimmer of a smile, a spark in his eyes.

Nada. The guy had to be a poker player, and a damn good one at that.

"What do you think?" She hated having to ask, but his ominous silence was giving her bad vibes.

He steepled his fingers, rested them on his chest, his gaze penetrating. He was studying her, almost sizing her up.

"I think you'll do nicely."

Relief made her knees wobble a tad, but Poppy couldn't shake the feeling she was being sized up for more than her presentation skills. She hated how authoritative guys had the power to make or break someone, but for Sara's sake, she'd kowtow like the rest of his flunkies. "You liked my pitch?"

He nodded and muttered, "And the rest."

Resisting the urge to happy dance after nailing a lucrative account that would go a long way to saving Sara's business, she sat opposite him and shut down her presentation. "I'll email you a quote with a complete breakdown of costs your twenty grand will cover."

"Fine," he said, his stare unwavering and seriously starting to unnerve her. "Do you have a venue in mind?"

Who did he think she was, Wonder Woman? She'd barely had time to put her presentation together after he'd summoned her, let alone research prospective venues.

She'd have to wing it. "I was waiting to get an idea of crowd size before following up with venues."

"Smart." Then why did she feel the opposite the longer he continued to study her?

There was something going on here, something beyond the initial buzz of attraction. His steady stare wasn't sexual — far from it. It was almost...predatory, as though he was a giant shark eyeing an itty-bitty flounder.

He stood and beckoned her closer. "We should check out some venues."

An order, not a request. Corporate hotshots like him were used to their demands being obeyed. And for the next few weeks, or however long it took to plan this party and run it, she'd have to do what he said. Within reason.

"I can do that online. Or I can schedule a return visit—"

"Now," he said, glancing at his watch. "We can grab some dinner, then check out the hotel function rooms."

She didn't want to have dinner with him, didn't want to be studied for one second longer than she had to. But it made sense to see the venues firsthand rather than online, and doing it now would save her a return trip. Though it wouldn't be half bad on that jet.

"Sounds good." She slid her tablet into her satchel and stood.

"I'll have my executive assistant call ahead and schedule it."

He strode toward his desk, power in motion, and she had to admit the combination of determination and authority, and the ease with which he wielded it, was pretty damned hot. She didn't go for suits, preferred her guys a little rough around the edges, but there was something about Beck Blackwood that appealed on a visceral level.

He'd be great fling material...if she ever lost her mind

and risked sleeping with an important business contact. As if. She'd nailed the first step, winning the pitch. If she could do the same with the party, news would spread and Divorce Diva Daily would be in demand. Yeah, she'd throw a divorce party like this town had never seen before. And that meant keeping her X-rated thoughts about Beck to herself.

"Done. Simone will arrange some viewing times in a few hours and make a dinner reservation." He snagged his jacket off the back of the chair and hooked it over his shoulder, looking executive and commanding and sexy at the same time.

Her hands-off resolution would be sorely tested. "Have to say, Poppy, I'm impressed." He had that penetrating stare going on again.

She gripped her bag tighter. "Thanks."

"So impressed, I have another business proposition for you later." His mouth eased into a slow grin and rather than easing her tension it ratcheted up.

"Great." Her inner diva did an exultant fist-pump.

"I hope you think so." But as he placed his hand in the small of her back to propel her toward the door, she couldn't shake the feeling this proposition would be more than she bargained for.

BECK HAD IMPECCABLE TIMING.

He carefully weighed decisions, analyzing all angles, before taking a metaphorical plunge.

He never wanted to be like his impulsive parents, who'd chased the next thrill, the next high.

Being rash ended in disaster, so the moment the idea to

have Poppy as his wife ignited, he'd mentally listed the pros and cons.

Pros: Amenable to business dealings. Intelligent. Attractive. Articulate. Professional. Suburban background. No skeletons. Not an acquaintance so no risk of emotional involvement.

Cons: ???

Hmm...looked like there wasn't one good reason to keep Poppy Collins from becoming the wife he needed.

Now he had to convince her.

"Dinner was sensational, but I'm so full I can hardly move." Poppy patted her stomach, drawing his gaze to the way the crimson silk draped her torso and clung to her breasts. The ruby color highlighted her vibrancy, deepening the lowlights in the shiny brunette tumble around her shoulders, bringing out the golden flecks in her eyes.

It illuminated her like a beacon, drawing the gaze of every guy in the room, and it vindicated his choice. She'd lost the jacket halfway through dinner and his triple-baked goat's cheese soufflé and anchovy-studded veal loin served with truffle polenta had morphed from sublime to tasteless in a second.

She was one of those rare women who managed to appear classy yet sexy, elegant yet down-to-earth, and she'd be perfect to convince the investors that Beck Blackwood was trustworthy and responsible.

"What do you think of this place?" His arm swept wide, encompassing the rooftop bar of the Blackwood, one of his company's finest hotels.

"It's perfect." Her eyes glittered with excitement as she gripped the metal railing and leaned forward, her hair rippling behind her like russet velvet in the cool night breeze. "Like being on top of the world."

"Best place to be," he said, joining her at the railing, their elbows inadvertently touching.

She didn't pull away and he wondered if she felt the sizzle, like an invisible thread tugging them together. He'd dated extensively but hadn't had this buzz often. It was heady, addictive, the kind of thrill that made a guy want to wind his hands through her hair, tug her closer, and kiss her senseless.

Later. After she'd agreed to his terms. And he had no doubt she would. He intended on making her an offer she couldn't refuse. But first he had to confirm his suspicions. "You mentioned your sister is the party planner and you're just filling in?"

"Uh-huh." Her casual response didn't fool him, not when she'd tightened her grip on the railing so that her knuckles stood out.

"Then why isn't there a mention of her on your website?"

A long pause, where she probably scrambled for an excuse to throw him off track. Not likely. He wasn't the type to give up, as she'd soon find out.

"She's taking a break."

"So you removed her from the website?" He shook his head. "I don't think so."

"What are you saying?" To her credit, she released the railing and swiveled to face him, chin tilted up in defiance.

"That you're hiding something linked to her Party Hard business, and I don't like signing off twenty grand to a potential charlatan."

She puffed up like an outraged bullfrog, managing to look indignant and gloriously sexy at the same time. "What sort of a businessman are you? You said I had the job. We're looking at freaking venues, and you can't back out now—"

"Hold on to your party poppers. I'm just protecting my investment." He laid a hand on her forearm, felt a tremor, and thought better of it. This deal would be complicated enough without his blood heading south. "If you want this job, I expect full disclosure."

"You're blackmailing me again?" Her lips parted in incredulity.

Not yet, but the night was young. "Up to you. Tell me the truth or I walk."

"Fine." But it wasn't, as she glared at him through narrowed eyes. "Sara's marriage fell apart, she's suffering from clinical depression, and her business, Party Hard, is on the brink of collapse. I stepped in, but the party planning biz in Provost isn't so hot these days, especially when word got out about her breakdown. And it doesn't help that her rat bastard ex is swanning around town like he owns the place, so people assume she did something wrong and that's why he left, and they back off from the business, too."

"Harsh." She nodded, worrying her bottom lip with her top teeth, the first sign of vulnerability. "While Provost is technically outer suburbia, it's like living in a small town."

"With a small-town mentality?" Now he was getting a clearer picture. Marketing whiz from LA steps in to save her sister's business but needs to keep it low key. Still didn't explain the lack of contact details and her obsession with anonymity.

"Exactly." She hesitated, as if weighing her next words. "Divorce parties wouldn't be the done thing in Provost—too conservative—so I set up Divorce Diva Daily as a separate entity from Party Hard. It's a potentially lucrative adjunct but I can't have anyone discovering my identity and the link to Party Hard."

She sighed. "Plus Sara's gone through a tough time

accepting her impending divorce, so I don't want to rub her face in it. She's fragile right now and couldn't handle it."

"I see."

"Do you? Because if word gets out, Sara will freak..." She shook her head, the sudden bleakness twisting her mouth making him want to kiss it all better. "I owe Sara and I'll do whatever it takes to save her business."

And just like that, she gave him the opportunity to outline his plan.

"Anything?"

"Within reason." Her eyebrow raised an infinitesimal millimeter.

"You're in luck, because I have another business proposition for you."

"What is it?" Curiosity lit her eyes.

He took a step closer, instantly enveloped in her tempting floral fragrance, enjoying the faintest flicker of inquisitiveness in her eyes. "Simple."

He snagged a strand of her hair, wound it around his finger, and tugged gently.

"Marry me."

SIX

Divorce Diva Daily recommends:
Playlist: "Fighter" by Christina Aguilera
Movie: Better Off Dead
Cocktail: Knockout Punch

"You're out of your freaking mind." Poppy placed her palms on Beck's chest and shoved, hard.

Considering the wall-to-wall muscle flexing imperceptibly beneath designer cotton, it was no surprise he didn't budge.

"Just hear me out—"

"No." She tried to back away but he had her cornered, railing at her back, lunatic at her front. "I'll scream."

He laughed. "Go ahead. I'm sure the gamblers fifty-four stories below will rush to your aid."

She swore.

He laughed harder. "It's the perfect business arrangement. I need a wife. You need money to save your sister's business, correct?"

"I don't need money that desperately," she muttered, wishing he'd get the hell out of her way.

He was too close, too intimidating, too everything, and she couldn't breathe.

In the seconds it took to process his outlandish proposal, a small part of her wondered what it would entail.

"A significant amount of money could make your problems go away."

She glared at his throat in response, annoyed when the sliver of bronzed skin visible between his lapels made her wonder if he was that tanned all over.

"How much do you need to get Party Hard into the black?"

Damn him for his persistence. Against her better judgment he'd piqued her interest. Hearing those words in the same sentence—Party Hard, into the black—sounded pretty damned good.

What if she could not only save Sara's business, but set her up so she wouldn't have to rush back to work? What if Sara could take her time recovering in the knowledge she had enough money to cover overheads, costs, and then some? She knew Sara worried about the business, even if she said she didn't. Her sis had always been an overachiever, setting a good example to make up for the emotional shortfalls of their parents. Failure didn't sit well with Sara, never had, and the fact her marriage had failed had been the catalyst for an underlying chemical imbalance they'd never known about.

"How much?"

"Five hundred thousand dollars." She threw it out there

as a taunt, wanting to shock him as much as he'd shocked her with his bizarre proposal.

"Done."

"What?" Dread slithered down her spine.

He reached out and gripped her upper arms, and she was too shell-shocked to pull away. "Let me make this simple for you. Investors are angsty because of an incident that tarnished my company's reputation recently. I need their backing for a major deal and they won't give it because they see me as some lecherous playboy heading a den of iniquity."

His grip eased but she didn't move away, the sincerity in his tone getting through to her like nothing else could. Wouldn't hurt to hear him out before she told him where he could stick his crazy offer.

"Being married to an intelligent, beautiful, suburban woman will give me the respectability I need to nail this deal." He splayed his fingers, the brush of his fingertips through the silk of her shirt setting off a static buzz. "And you get to save your sister's business single-handedly. Win-win."

Speechless, she shook her head. "My deal gets done. Then we go our separate ways."

Damn him for making it sound so logical, so easy, while she still reeled. Hotshot guys were used to wielding power and money to get what they wanted, but marriage? Beck Blackwood was either seriously delusional, seriously arrogant, or a staggering combination of both.

She rolled her eyes. "That'd be great publicity, throwing my own divorce party."

He missed her sarcasm when he smiled, and his lack of superciliousness impressed. "Yeah, think how business would boom."

"Except for the part where I need to remain anonymous."

"Hey, with the amount of money you'd be depositing in your sister's account, who cares if the whole damn town doesn't knock on her door again?"

Good point. "Okay, on the off chance I lose my mind and consider this for longer than one second, how exactly would it work?"

"Logistics are my forte."

She hated his triumphant grin almost as much as she hated herself for considering this. What kind of crazy person married another for money? Actually, when she phrased it like that, it didn't seem so bizarre at all. People did it every day: for the security and high life money could bring. At least she'd be doing it for an altruistic cause.

But *married*? She was the least romantic person she knew and the whole white dress/man of her dreams had never been high on her to-do list. Marriages made people do dumb things—she'd seen that firsthand with her sister. As for love? Waste of time. Love faded, gave way to antipathy at best, derision at worst. Why take the risk?

She'd never met anyone who remotely piqued her interest long enough to consider falling in love, never had the ridiculous tummy free-fall depicted in chick flicks.

In a way, a business marriage would suit her purposes nicely. No fuss, no muss.

And the kicker, she would save Sara in the process. Win-win indeed.

"I'd take care of everything. Marriage license, ceremony, reception."

She wrinkled her nose. "We'd have to go through the charade of a reception?"

"This marriage has to look real to my investors, otherwise we're wasting our time." His quick look away was the first time she'd seen him anything other than one hundred percent confident in his outlandish scheme. "We can keep the ceremony quiet but the reception will have to be big."

"How big?"

"I'm a prominent businessman and this deal I'm trying to nail will take Blackwood Enterprises nationwide." He shrugged. "You do the math."

If considering this zany idea didn't make her belly churn, the thought of pretending in front of hundreds did the trick. "You're really serious about this?" She searched his face for answers to questions she could barely formulate.

"I don't propose marriage to every woman I meet." His wry grin alleviated the tension lines bracketing his mouth but did little for the wariness clouding his eyes.

She knew the feeling. Wary didn't come close to how she was feeling. Try floundering, confused, and freaking petrified. "What about living arrangements? The legalities of terminating after a year? Appearing in public together? Would there be other functions with your investors—"

"Standard prenup to facilitate easy termination. As for the rest, this marriage needs to look real in every way." His gaze locked on hers, mesmerizing and challenging, daring her to ask how real.

Heat licked her veins at the thought of how far she could go to make this marriage authentic; if she lost her mind. "I guess my assistant, Ashlee, could man the Provost office and I could consult as needed while continuing to run Divorce Diva Daily online."

"You'd continue with that?"

"Of course. Your cash injection isn't going to last forever. Besides, I'd be lousy as a trophy wife."

"Oh, I don't know. I can see you lounging around poolside in a black bikini...thong, of course—"

"Dream on."

"I'm doing plenty of that." He stepped into her personal space, crowding her, bamboozling her.

She couldn't think with him so close, let alone breathe, her senses bombarded by his nearness, his crisp aftershave, his heat. So much heat, radiating off him like a furnace and making her want to lean into him.

"You know this marriage won't be that real, right?" She regretted the question the instant it slipped from her lips as his eyes flared with fire. She should've known better than to challenge a go-getter.

"Who are you trying to convince?" His smoldering gaze dipped to her lips. "Because from where I'm standing, making this marriage appear real in every way is my number one priority."

Poppy couldn't breathe, couldn't think, his preposterous proposal reverberating through her head until she wanted to bang it against the wall. He made a fake marriage sound logical, but could she really pretend to be this guy's wife?

Beck Blackwood encapsulated everything she despised: arrogant, commanding, bossy. Being shackled to him, albeit for a good cause, would be insufferable. But she couldn't lose out on the twenty grand for his buddy's party, so she better couch her refusal wisely.

"Thanks for the offer, and I appreciate you discussing how this would pan out, but I'm afraid my answer's no."

Shock flared in his eyes before he blinked. When he reopened them, the eerily cool green almost sent a shiver of trepidation down her spine. "And I'm afraid you've misunderstood me."

Huh?

"I need a wife ASAP or I'm screwed. You need to protect your sister and I can help do that. Marriage is a speedy resolution for us both."

Uh-oh. His steely stare wasn't that of an altruistic man. It was the "You'll do as I say or else" stare that foreshadowed a threat. Plus he didn't mention the money to save Sara's business. He'd said protect. What did he mean?

She shook her head. "Sorry. Not interested—"

"It's quite simple. Either you marry me or I let slip your precious secret." His silky tone raised the hairs on the nape of her neck. "And I'm sure you wouldn't want your sister to hear you're touting divorce in her condition."

He was *blackmailing* her into marriage? Red spots of rage danced before her eyes and she almost swayed, wishing she could punch him.

How many times had she seen guys like him coerce their way in and out of situations? Her dad had been a classic example, buying his way into the local country club, paying off a patient who threatened to go to the media when she wasn't happy with his work, throwing lavish gifts at her to assuage his guilt at being a lousy dad.

His friends had been the same, too, assuming money gave them the right to control anything and anyone. It made her sick, and now she could add Beck Blackwood to the Rich Pricks Society.

Poppy dragged in several deep breaths, wisely waiting until the red spots faded before speaking. "I take it planning the party's off the table if I refuse?"

"Smart girl." He took a step closer and she forced her feet not to instinctively back away. "So what's it going to be?"

"Honestly? I'm over the blackmail routine you have

down-pat." She tilted her head up to eyeball him. "So you can take your dumbass proposal and—"

He kissed her, effectively shutting her up. A novel silencing technique, one she had no intention of submitting to. But as her brain sent a snappy message to her knee—aim for the groin—a strange thing happened.

"Please," he murmured against her mouth. "This deal is everything to me."

She heard a hint of vulnerability beneath his surprisingly honest declaration and it resonated like nothing else. She knew the kind of desperation that made people do crazy things, was doing it for Sara in turning up here in the first place.

"I can't—"

He coaxed her lips apart, confident and demanding and oh so delicious. There was no sweet seduction, no hesitation, as he plied her with a skill that left her breathless and reluctantly clinging to him.

She'd never been the helpless female type, taking as good as she got, but there was something about Beck's take-charge attitude that made her weak-kneed and a little off-kilter.

His arms slid around her waist and pulled her flush against his erection at the same time his tongue invaded her mouth, sending a jolt of pure lust shooting to her core.

She shouldn't want him, shouldn't want this...whatever this was.

He plundered her mouth, long, hot, moist kisses that had her boneless and mindless with desire, until all she could do was sag against him, soft and pliant and wanting. So much wanting.

An eternity later his lips eased away, lingering long

enough to place a surprisingly sweet kiss on the corner of her mouth.

"One last time." He traced her bottom lip with a fingertip, the residual tingle from his kiss intensifying, as he stared at her with the determination of a guy used to getting his own way. "Marry me?"

She wanted to say no. She wanted to tell him where he could stick his proposal. But he'd left her no choice. Sara had been the only parent she'd ever known, and now it was Poppy's turn to do the protecting. She owed Sara and she'd do whatever it took, including giving in to this incredibly infuriating guy.

Hating how he'd bullied her into this, hating herself for succumbing to that scintillating kiss more, she nodded, a reluctant "Yeah" tumbling from her lips a second before he claimed them again.

∽

"YOU'RE NOT WEARING HEELS." Ashlee stared at Poppy's feet, her eyes wide. "Did you botch the Blackwood pitch?" She placed a hand on Poppy's forehead. "Fever? Not feeling well?"

With a resigned sigh, Poppy flopped onto the ergonomic chair and propped her ballet-flat clad feet on the desk. "Leave me alone, I'm exhausted."

"Ah...it's like that."

"Like what?"

"Would The Hottie have anything to do with your exhaustion?" Ashlee rubbed her hands together. "Spill."

Poppy winced behind her sunglasses. Yeah, Beck Blackwood had everything to do with her bone-deep tiredness.

She hadn't slept all night. It had little to do with the

exceptional espresso she'd drunk on the jet before touching down just after midnight, and everything to do with what he'd done.

Blackmailed her into marriage. And used his damned kissing skill to seduce her into saying yes.

Okay, so she hadn't put up much of a fight once her hormones overrode her anger but jeez, did he have to be so goddamned sexy? As a fury-diffuser and distracting technique, his kisses had done the trick, and once they'd broken the lip-lock and come up for air, they'd sat down and worked out the logistics—what the prenup entailed, a generous settlement of the half-a-million figure she'd thrown at him expecting refusal, and the terms of their business arrangement.

That's what this marriage was—a business arrangement between two people with no romantic aspirations or illusions, two insane people who'd do anything to reach their goals. She should be proud of herself for going this far for Sara. Instead, all she could think was *What the hell have I done?*

"Where do I start?" Poppy took a deep breath and blew it out, glad she could trust Ashlee. She couldn't talk to Sara, not about this, and if she didn't tell someone, she'd burst. "The part where he agreed to my pitch?"

Ashlee squealed and clapped her hands like a hyperactive kid.

"Or the part where I agreed to marry him?"

Ashlee collapsed into the seat opposite, her mouth a perfect O as she stared at Poppy as if she'd announced she was a finalist for a reality TV show.

"Crazy, huh?"

Ashlee's lips moved but no words came out.

"He needs a wife for business, I need money to save

Sara's business, so apparently we're a good fit." Poppy resisted the urge to squirm in her seat at the memory of exactly how well they fit together.

When he had her backed up against that wall, his hands everywhere, she'd been so turned on she could've gotten naked right there and then. Funny how fast thoughts of kneeing him in the groin had turned to wanting to grope his groin. "It's a temporary arrangement. Twelve months, tops. Not so bad."

The silence grated on her nerves. "Say something."

"Are you nuts?" Ashlee shook her head, cleared her throat. "Did he slip you a roofie? Were you drunk and dreamed up this crazy idea?" She pointed at Poppy's sunglasses. "And take those off. I can't see your eyes."

"So?"

"I can't see if you're being serious or getting back at me for borrowing your fave stilettos that one time."

"Twice." Poppy slid her sunglasses off and Ashlee recoiled.

"Ballet flats and no mascara? Gross. You're either sick or The Hottie kept you up all night. Before he proposed, that is." Ashlee rolled her eyes and folded her arms, less than impressed with what she assumed was her fabricated story. "What really happened?"

"I told you." Her serious tone took a few seconds to penetrate Ashlee's disbelief, as her friend went from dubious to dumb-founded. "You're marrying the guy?"

Ashlee made it sound like she was heading on a one-way trip to Mars on a defective shuttle.

"Yeah, it's good business sense."

"Good business sense," Ashlee parroted before smacking her forehead. "What do you think this is, a freaking romance novel? Fictional characters get married for convenience, not people in real life. And certainly not you."

"Why not?"

"Because you're not the marrying kind." Ashlee held up her left hand and pointed to the snazzy carats on her ring finger. "Remember what you told me when Craig proposed?"

Yeah, Poppy remembered, and at the time she'd meant every word of her anti-marriage spiel. She'd been happy for her friend, but when Ashlee had gushed Poppy would be next, she'd stated in no uncertain terms why she wouldn't be. Didn't make sense. Humans weren't meant to be monogamous for life, and from the many marriages she'd witnessed over the years, she could count the ones that survived with two truly happy partners on one hand.

It was why this arrangement with Beck Blackwood was the perfect solution to her problems. No dreams of happily ever after to cloud her judgment. Sara got a cool half a million and Poppy went some way toward repaying the massive emotional debt she owed her only sibling.

Best reason for marriage she could think of. "I'm doing the right thing, Ash, but I need your help."

"I won't be party to this charade—"

"You will be if you want to keep your job."

Damn, why had she blurted that? Probably her dear husband-to-be rubbing off on her with his blackmail routine. Tears pooled in Ashlee's eyes and Poppy reached across the desk to pat her hand. "Sorry, hon, I'm a little stressed."

"And a lot crazy," Ashlee muttered, shaking her head. "You're seriously going to marry this guy?"

"Yeah, and I need you to hold down the fort here while I shack up with him in Vegas."

"You'll be living with The Hottie?" For the first time

since Poppy had announced her plans, the old matchmaking spark flickered to life in Ashlee's eyes.

"That's what married people do."

The glint intensified. "Married people also do other stuff, so does that mean you and he…" She made a rather crude action with her finger and opposing fist, and Poppy blushed.

"None of your business."

"You are!" Ashlee jabbed an accusatory finger in her direction. "How far did you go last night to seal this deal?"

"Not that far," Poppy said, wondering what she would've done if Beck had taken those kisses further. She might have despised him for leaving her no choice but to agree to his proposal, but her body? Having no such qualms. She dated. She liked sex. But how he'd turned her on last night with a mere makeout session? Yowza.

"We've got a lot to get through today—"

"When are you getting married?"

"Next week." It sounded ludicrous even to her ears and Ashlee's squeal didn't help.

"I better be invited."

"I was hoping you'd be a witness."

"Done." Ashlee dashed a hand across her suspiciously moist eyes. "I can't believe you're getting married."

She wasn't the only one. This time next week Poppy would be Mrs. Beck Blackwood.

How far the diva had fallen. "Neither can I, Ash. Neither can I."

SEVEN

Divorce Diva Daily recommends:
Playlist: "Trouble" by Pink
Movie: It's Complicated
Cocktail: Hot Dream

Poppy knew she was in a bad way when she couldn't raise a chuckle after penning her funniest blog yet. She knew why she wasn't in the mood for smiling, too.

Sara.

Poppy had to tell her sis about her upcoming nuptials. It wouldn't be pretty. Sara took her parenting role seriously. Sara had been the one to take her training-bra shopping, to pick her up from the prom when that dork Mick Miller dumped her, to cruise down to San Diego in her first car.

Guess she should've been grateful that Rozelle and Earl tore themselves away from their surgery long enough to attend her graduation. Her folks had loved her in their own way—a narcissist, absentee way—and Sara had willingly picked up the slack.

Sara had always been the responsible one: going to college, marrying a rich guy from a good family, buying the picket fence house. It had made it all the harder to watch when Sara's dream came crashing down, and while her sister was getting stronger every day, Poppy couldn't equate the morose waif now with the sister who ate brownies for breakfast and laughed the longest.

Poppy had considered not telling her until after the wedding but couldn't risk her finding out via the media. Beck Blackwood was hot property in Vegas; she couldn't take the chance. It'd be hard enough for Sara to believe in this marriage, and the last thing she needed was to add to her doubts.

The marriage had to appear real in every way for Sara not to catch on to her motivation. That was all Poppy needed, for Sara to discover the real reason she was getting married and blame herself. No way Poppy would let that happen. She had it all figured out: play up the romance angle, downplay her sketchy knowledge of her groom. And thank the powers that be at the clinic for their "No checking out early" policy. While they allowed freedom of day trips once a client had stabilized, they operated under strict rehab rules, and according to her therapist, Sara wasn't ready to leave. Which made Poppy's job of playing the adoring, blushing bride all that easier. Although she may have been able to fool a bunch of Beck's business cronies, she couldn't have fooled Sara if she saw the two of them at some makeshift altar.

No, it was easier this way. Sara would be none the wiser and when Poppy's marriage "fell apart" at a later date, her sis would be strong enough to handle it.

Poppy had it all figured out. Except the part where Beck had emailed her details of the wedding. She'd expected him to go for Vegas glitz in one of Blackwood's luxurious hotels with an entourage of movers and shakers in tow. What she hadn't expected? To buy a dress for a low-key desert wedding near his home in Red Rock Canyon.

With his designer suits and slick attitude, she didn't expect him to give a crap about the desert, let alone live there. It rattled her, how much she didn't know about her husband-to-be. Then again, she had time to discover all she needed to know.

And five hundred grand was a damned good incentive to figure him out.

Poppy turned into the clinic's driveway, hit the intercom button, stared into the video cam, gave her name, and waited to be buzzed through.

As the wrought-iron gates swung open she pulled into the nearest parking spot, took a few steadying breaths, and readied herself to confront her sister. Zenza Clinic may have looked low key with its lush lawns, manicured garden beds, and hotel lobby entrance, but having to sign in and wear a visitor's lanyard before being buzzed through electronically locked doors reinforced the reality that her sister was virtually a prisoner here by choice.

Poppy smiled at the head nurse on her way toward Sara's room, surprised when the nurse shook her head and beckoned her over.

"Just so you know, she's not having a great day."

Poppy's heart sank. "Did anything set her off?"

The nurse shrugged. "She was doing some surfing online, seemed to withdraw after that."

"Okay, thanks for the heads up."

So much for her grand plan to break the news gently.

She'd seen these relapses before, where all Sara wanted to do was relax in her room listening to New Age pan flutes. After Poppy divulged the news of her upcoming nuptials, a whole orchestra of woodwind wouldn't soothe her.

She paused outside Sara's door, rolling her shoulders and stretching her neck from side to side. It didn't alleviate her tension, and she braced for an interrogation of mammoth proportions. She knocked, waited for the faint "Come in" before entering.

The first thing she noticed was the drawn blinds on a gorgeous spring day. The second, the faintest strains of piped music. Freaking flutes.

Yep, this would be a crap-tastic day.

"Hey, Sara." Poppy's chirpiness sounded forced even to her ears. "How are you?"

"Okay." Sara tolerated her hug with the barest of squeezes in return.

Poppy perched on the end of the bed, opposite the sofa where Sara sat like a beautiful, delicate statue: auburn hair shiny, make-up perfect, turquoise designer yoga pants and matching hoodie, but an eerily blank expression and a glassy stare. "What's up?"

"Divorce."

Uh-oh. "Has Wayne filed—"

"Not yet." Sara shook her head. "I was feeling really hyped this morning, best I've felt in ages, so I jumped online to scope out the competition, see how business is doing."

Fingers of foreboding pinched the back of Poppy's neck and she rubbed it.

"Know what I found? A website promoting divorce parties." Sara absentmindedly plucked at the string on her velour hoodie. "Some diva saying they're the next greatest thing...can you imagine someone making money from people's misery?"

Shit. And Poppy had been worried about Sara discovering the real reason behind her fake marriage. Looked like she had more important things to worry about.

"You never considered them for Party Hard?"

"No freaking way." Sara paused, sniffled. "Not after Wayne left..."

Ah hell, just what she needed, Sara to lament her lousy husband at length.

"Could be the way to go once yours is final. Put the past behind—"

"I still love him," Sara whispered, and Poppy's heart turned over in sympathy. Little wonder Sara was having a hard time dealing with depression when she was still mooning over The Pain.

"Know what I think? Never say never. Divorce parties are the latest rage, they'd rake in a fortune for Party Hard—"

"I don't want to talk about it."

"Uh, okay."

Now more than ever she needed to preserve the anonymity of Divorce Diva Daily. Last thing her sis needed was to learn of Party Hard's offshoot. "I've got some news."

"Yeah?" Sara didn't look at her, closing her eyes and resting her head against the back of the sofa like the simple act of holding up her body was too much.

"I'm getting married."

"What?" Sara's eyelids snapped open and she sat bolt upright. The incredulous look Sara shot her? The same one she'd used to great effect when Poppy had made the mistake of divulging her desire for a tattoo of a boy band under her navel at sixteen.

"Tomorrow. In Vegas."

"You're pregnant?" Sara glared at her belly like she expected alien spawn to suddenly explode out of it.

"Uh-uh."

"Then why?" When Sara's gaze met hers, the unexpected anguish hit her hard. She'd expected her sister to be shocked. She hadn't expected the pain.

Well aware lying to her sister would be the hardest thing she'd ever have to do, Poppy took a deep breath and blew it out. "Because the time is right."

Boy, was it ever. Save the business, save her sister's sanity.

"But who is this guy? Why Vegas? Why now?" Confusion added to the hurt in Sara's eyes. "You know I can't come."

"I thought maybe it'll be easier this way."

"All weddings don't make me depressed, only mine."

Poppy smiled, impressed at her sister's acerbic wit and ability to make a joke out of something so obviously painful. "We've known each other a while, didn't see any point in waiting."

She hoped lightning wouldn't strike her down. "He's the old-fashioned type and kept badgering me to get hitched, so I finally said yes."

"But who is he and why haven't you mentioned him?" Great time for her sis to gain clarity.

"Beck Blackwood. He's CEO of a big construction company based in Vegas." She glanced skyward, expecting to see a stray bolt at any time. "I haven't mentioned him because you've been dealing with a lot of stuff. And I didn't want to gush about how great he is while you've been coming to terms with Wayne's departure."

"But you've always been anti-marriage." Sara's eyes narrowed. "What makes this guy so special?"

Poppy would have to make this sound convincing and get the hell out of there, because she had a feeling the longer she stayed, the harder it'd be to skirt around Sara's increasingly probing questions.

"He's amazing. Thoughtful"—to the extent he thought she'd want to marry him for money—"kind"—he better be or she'd neuter him—"and absolutely gorgeous." One truth out of three ain't bad. "He'd do anything for me." Including blackmail and flinging five hundred big ones her way to get her to jump to his tune. "And I want to be with him, so why wait?"

For some inexplicable reason, her last reason brought a lump to her throat.

What would it be like to have a guy like Beck propose marriage for real? Not for altruism, but because he had to be with her? She'd never experience it, not in this lifetime. And while she had turned her back on love and all it entailed by choice, that didn't mean she didn't have a heart.

"Wow." Some of the accusatory gleam faded from Sara's suspicious stare. "This guy must be something to get you to fall this hard."

"He's something, all right." At last, one hundred percent truth. "Can't wait for you to meet him." *Sometime next century.*

Sara's wobbly smile made her heart ache. "Be happy, Pops, because divorce is a bitch."

Didn't she know it. Ironic. In her case, it was the part of the marriage she was looking forward to the most.

∞

WHEN BECK HAD a goal in sight, he wanted to achieve it ASAP.

No stalling, no delays. He wanted to get this over with as he caught sight of Poppy strolling toward him in a stunning wedding dress. Classy. Elegant. Sexy.

The satin hugged her curves and ended mid-calf while the tops of her breasts peeped enticingly over the strapless crystal-beaded bodice. Her hair tumbled in loose spiral curls to her shoulder, held back from her face with a mini diamanté tiara, a gossamer-thin veil trailing to the floor behind her.

That's when he noticed her shoes. Crimson. Sparkly. Impossibly high. The same memorable color as the shirt she'd worn to her pitch, the color he couldn't get out of his head, the color he'd forever associate with her.

Poppy. She didn't stroll down the makeshift aisle, she strutted, her gaze locked on his, daring and defiant.

And he'd never been so turned on in all his life. Damn it, marrying this woman was part of a well-thought-out, precisely executed business plan, and he couldn't afford to screw it up. Which was exactly what would happen if he started thinking about consummation.

He could do sex without strings, but in his experience, women equated the bedroom with emotion and romance. No way in hell would he mess this up by complicating their arrangement with sex. Despite the raging desire to do just that.

"Nice tux." She stopped a foot away and smoothed his lapels, close enough he could smell her intoxicating floral fragrance.

"Nice shoes," he said, unable to resist ducking down to place a kiss just shy of her ruby-slicked lips.

"In case you hadn't noticed, I always wear a splash of red." Her strangely lopsided smile told him she wasn't quite as confident as she made out. "Corny namesake."

"I think it's sexy." He touched her cheek, a fleeting gesture that rattled him as much as it did her, if the sudden widening of her eyes was any indication.

He had no idea how long they stood there, gazes locked, his hand caressing her cheek, and if it hadn't been for the minister clearing his throat he would've swept her into his arms and kissed her silly. To eradicate her doubts, of course. Nothing at all to do with the burning, relentless desire to taste her again.

"Shall we begin?"

"You ready?" He grasped her hand and squeezed. Wild-eyed, she darted a look over her shoulder and for a horrifying second he thought she'd bolt.

"We need to do this." He felt like a jerk for badgering her. How desperate must she be to save her sister's business to marry a stranger? Her devotion impressed him and if she could bring one-tenth of that loyalty to this marriage, enough to impress the investors this sham was real, he'd be happy.

She dragged in a few deep breaths and he saw the moment her resolution hardened. Her head tilted up and she nodded. "Let's do it."

The vows passed in a blur of echoed verses, agreeing to love, honor, and obey. Empty words, empty promises, and how far he'd go to achieve his goal hit home when he looked into her eyes and said, "I do."

For in that moment, everything faded: the minister, their witnesses Lou and Ashlee, and the stunning backdrop of the red rocks he called home.

He'd just pledged himself to a woman he barely knew. A smart business choice, one that would gain him the national recognition he craved. Then why the soul-deep niggle he was getting in over his head?

"You may kiss the bride." The minister beamed as he snapped his ceremony book shut.

"Well, hotshot, what are you waiting for?" Her lips curved in a saucy smile, her sass too late in covering the sheen he'd glimpsed in her eyes. Hell, he couldn't handle waterworks. So he did the one thing he'd been desperate to do since he first laid eyes on her strutting up the aisle.

He swept her into his arms and kissed her.

EIGHT

Divorce Diva Daily recommends:
Playlist: "White Wedding" by Billy Idol
Movie: Love Actually
Cocktail: Bride's Cuss

Poppy knew she shouldn't play with fire.

Taunting a guy like Beck would only ever have one outcome. With him on top.

Guys like him never lost. Whatever they gambled on, they won. Every time. Success bred success and while she'd been happy with her life, it wasn't until the moment the minister had pronounced them husband and wife that reality hit.

She'd married a virtual stranger. Now that she'd done the deed, a million doubts assailed her. How could she pretend to play the adoring wife in front of his business colleagues? Play the adoring wife in front of his business colleagues? Remain immune to his charms?

Therein lay her real concern—that the moment she'd seen him at the end of the makeshift aisle, mouthwateringly, wickedly gorgeous in a tux, silhouetted against the stark beauty of Red Rock Canyon, her heart had given an uncomfortable squirm and she recognized it for what it was. A reminder that despite the fact she should hate him for blackmailing her into this farce, she could fall into bed with this guy given half a chance.

So daring him to kiss her? Probably not a great idea.

"Wow." Ashlee snagged her arm and dragged her a safe distance from where Beck and Lou were in deep conversation. "You sure you're faking it? Because from where I was standing, you two look seriously into each other."

"Pheromones."

As Beck glanced her way with a crooked half smile that elicited an answering twang deep within, some of those damn hormones set up a party in regions best left ignored for now.

"Just be careful, hon."

"Of?"

Ashlee hesitated. "The Hottie isn't a keeper. He'll break your heart."

"No danger of that happening. This is business, remember?"

As Beck strolled toward her, jacket slung over his shoulder, bow tie askance, top button of his ivory dress shirt unbuttoned, piercing green eyes with a wicked glint, she knew without a doubt she'd be the one having to remember this marriage was all business.

"Whatever you say, sweetie." Ashlee lowered her voice to a whisper. "But anything involving that guy's gonna be monkey business."

Wishful thinking. When Beck reached Poppy's side, he

slipped an arm around her waist like it was the most natural thing in the world. Sure, they had to keep up appearances—and he wasn't aware Ashlee knew the truth—but it made her feel more like a fraud than she already was, the pretense in front of her friend.

"Nice to meet you, Ashlee, and thanks for coming. Lou will take you back to town in the limo and we'll see you at the reception later."

"Sure thing." Ashlee practically simpered as she shook Beck's hand and moved away, mouthing Hottie over his shoulder at Poppy.

"What's with the grin?"

"Just so darned happy to be your wife," Poppy said, batting her eyelashes at him.

He laughed and tightened his grip around her waist. "You know that smart mouth of yours will get you into trouble one day?"

"Today if I'm lucky."

What was it with this guy that had her wanting to spar and parry and play word games? She shouldn't flirt with him unless people who needed convincing of the validity of this marriage surrounded them. It would only give him the wrong idea.

Which was what? The fact she had the hots for her husband big time?

Flustered, she rushed on. "Where are we going?"

"My place."

She didn't understand the reservation in his voice. She'd already dumped her stuff in his penthouse suite in Blackwood Towers. Wasn't as if she hadn't seen it.

"Good. It'll give us time to chill before the reception."

"Yeah." Tension pinched the corners of his mouth, his

fingers inadvertently digging into her waist. "You know how important the reception is, right?"

Ah, so that's what his funk was about. Making sure she played her part in front of his precious investors.

"I was the number one drama queen in high school."

He grimaced. "That's what I'm afraid of."

"That came out wrong." She patted his cheek. "I was a fabulous actress. Best Juliet ever."

"Wish you hadn't used the star-crossed lovers as an example."

"Don't be such a worrywart. Your investors will love me."

He eased away and she immediately missed his touch. Crazy.

His gaze traveled from her shoes upward in a slow, sensual sweep that left her skin tingling like he'd just caressed her. "You're amazing, you know that, right?"

She resisted the urge to squirm under his praise. "I found it in a boutique—"

"I'm not talking about the dress." For the first time since they'd met, the powerful aura he wore like a protective cloak fell away and she glimpsed a hint of genuine emotion beneath the tough-guy exterior. It undermined her more than his compliment.

"Not many women would put up with my blackmailing shit and go through all this for the sake of family." He touched her hand, and before she could second-guess herself, she intertwined her fingers with his. "Loyalty's important to me. And what you've demonstrated..." He raised her hand to his lips and kissed the back of it, sending a shiver of longing through her. "Let's just say I think we're going to make a good team for however long this marriage lasts."

And just like that, he ripped apart the cocoon of intimacy surrounding them.

He admired her loyalty. Whoop de-frikking-do. He made it sound like she was one of his valued employees. And that more than anything rammed home, despite his murmured platitudes and hot kisses and frequent touches, that this was a simple business transaction.

More of a concern? Why the hell did she care?

"Vegas is that way." Poppy pointed over her shoulder as Beck steered his Maserati in the opposite direction from which she'd arrived.

"We're not heading to Vegas." He floored it, kicking up a plume of red dust in the car's wake.

"But you said we're heading to your place."

"We are."

Ah...the mysterious desert home. She couldn't fathom his enigmatic expression as he drove like he had a pack of creditors on his tail.

"I'm surprised you own a place out here." She didn't mean to make it sound like he lived in the back of beyond, but that's how it must've sounded, judging by his scowl.

"The glitz of Vegas isn't me." He nodded at the majestic red rocks jutting skyward ahead of them. "This place is."

Poppy glanced around, trying to see the appeal. Grassy fields, various trees interspersed with desert, and those striking red rocks. She'd had no idea why he'd chosen Red Rock Canyon as the site to get married and hadn't really cared. She didn't believe in the institution, let alone worry about the location when there was nothing real about this marriage, bar the money.

But now, seeing Beck's tense expression, she wondered if there was more behind his location choice. "You like the desert?"

"What's not to like? Land forged under a shallow sea, buried for eons beneath sand dunes, then sculpted by rains and wind."

"I take it you were top of your class in geography."

The corners of his mouth twitched. "I come from a small desert town about a hundred miles from here. When I lobbed in Vegas and scored my first construction deal, I bought land in Red Rock Canyon. Thought it'd be the perfect commute, less than twenty miles from the Strip. Then work took over..." He shrugged, as if it meant little, but she wondered how a desert guy really felt being cooped up in the city. "I don't get out here very often."

"So why are we heading there when we need to get ready for the reception tonight?"

His silence unnerved her almost as much as the bleak glance he shot her before refocusing on the road. "Thought you might need a place to get away to if the going gets tough."

Okay, so that was thoughtful. It would be hard, keeping up the pretense of being happily married, but she figured they'd barely see each other anyway, what with his booming business and her managing Party Hard online for Sara.

Poppy could handle the odd occasion performing for his colleagues, but it would be wearing. She'd never been two-faced. What you saw was what you got with her, so playing Mrs. Blackwood would be a challenge. One she was certainly up for, for five hundred grand.

"Thanks, that sounds good."

Considering the way he'd shut her down in the limo on the night they'd met when she'd brought up family, she probably shouldn't go there. But he'd mentioned he'd grown up in the desert and surely she'd have to know stuff like his background for the sake of authenticity.

"You were raised out here?"

He grunted in response.

"I'll probably need to know a little about your family, in case I'm quizzed."

"My family is no secret. Tabloids did a spread on me when I first made it big. Mentioned my folks, how they died, that kind of thing." His hands gripped the steering wheel, his frigid tone warning her to back off. "Irrelevant now."

"Not to your wife."

He shot her a quick glare. "Checkerville's your typical small town. Rich folk, poor folk. We were the latter."

"We?"

"My parents. Pa." He jaw clenched, as if he didn't want to say anything more, so she waited.

"Nan died when Mom was young, so Pa raised her alone. He's a mechanic, she was working at the grocer. Then Dad rode into town."

She wanted to make a joke about cowboys but knew he'd clam up.

"According to Pa, Mom fell for Dad, Pa fell for his motorcycle. Dad had big dreams, but that's all they were. He talked the talk but couldn't hold down a job, let alone support a family. They had me nine months after they met. Dad packed us up, moved to Vegas."

His glower darkened, if that were possible. "Fell into his old crowd. Alcohol. Drugs. Mom was miserable, got hooked on the stuff. Apparently, they drifted back to Checkerville every time they were broke, which was often. We lived in a trailer on the outskirts of town. It was a hovel."

The longer he spoke in that flat, toneless voice, the more she wished she hadn't opened this proverbial can.

"They OD'd when I was seven. Shooting up together.

Bad batch of coke. After that, Pa took me in. So now you know."

She'd been so caught up in his disclosures she hadn't realized they'd pulled onto a side road leading to the biggest pair of wrought-iron gates she'd ever seen.

A guy like him would abhor pity, but she had to say something sympathetic. "Your Pa must be proud."

The lines fanning his eyes eased and she released a little relieved sigh.

"He's great. I don't get to see him often enough these days."

"He'd understand your work commitments."

"Yeah, but it's not good enough."

The tension had returned and she grabbed at the quickest change of subject, gesturing at the towering cream-rendered wall that stretched as far as she could see. "This your place?"

"No, it's Eldorado."

She smiled at his sarcasm as he grabbed a remote from the console and hit a button. The wall prevented her from seeing much and she wondered if his desert house would be as fancy as his hotels. Curious, she wriggled in her seat as the gates swung open to reveal a building that took her breath away.

"Wow," she said, not sure where to look first as he drove up the curving driveway to the front of the house. "Quite a house."

She used the term lightly, because this was no ordinary house.

A two-story Spanish-style hacienda sprawled across the high-walled block, surrounded by native gardens that accentuated the stark beauty of the terracotta mansion.

"You were expecting a shack?" She didn't know if he

was uncomfortable about divulging his past and was taking a dig to disguise his discomfort, so she let it slide.

"It's beautiful." She craned her neck as he pulled under a portico and cut the engine. "I love it."

His expression softened. "It's a great place to depressurize."

And she bet he needed to do plenty of that, considering the guy was worth billions.

Learning of his background only exacerbated her curiosity. How did a guy from the wrong side of the tracks make it big? He must've worked his ass off, and his self-made success only increased his hotness factor.

It also explained the rugged, rough around the edges thing he had going on. He wore his hair a little too long to be strictly conventional, wore his designer shirts with the top button perpetually undone.

She liked the subtle rebellions against conventional corporate. Very sexy.

"Come on, I'll give you the grand tour."

She slipped her shoes back on, feeling like a princess when he opened her door and took hold of her hand to help her out. Another thing that impressed: impeccable manners. He led her along a paved path toward the front door, which he unlocked with a fancy keycard.

"I'm not around much, so state of the art security."

He folded his arms, shoulders rigid, waiting for her to pass. No prizes for guessing he was still uptight after discussing his past in the car. Time to lighten the mood a little.

"Aren't you forgetting something?"

"What?"

"Does this look like a threshold to you?" She air-drew the outline of the door with her finger.

A spark of amusement lit his eyes. "So?"

"*Hello?*" She gestured at her dress, snagged her veil and waved it in his face. "New bride alert?"

Incredulous, he swatted her veil away. "You don't seriously expect me to carry you inside?"

"You don't seriously expect me to behave like a bride if you don't treat me like one."

He laughed, a genuine joyous sound that made her feel like hugging him so tight it hurt. "Never would've picked you as a stickler for tradition." He swept her into his arms. "Not with these shoes."

"What's wrong with my shoes?" She kicked a heel in the air, he dipped her, and she let out a squeal.

"If you're aiming for the come-get-me signal, they're working perfectly."

She couldn't think of a single smart-ass retort as his gaze swept upward from her shoes, lingered on her lips, and finally met her stare.

"So do you?" Her words came out as a whisper.

He inched closer until their lips were a hairsbreadth apart. "What?"

"Want to come get me?"

"What do you think?" He stepped over the threshold so damn fast her head spun. As he lowered her he kicked the door shut and backed her against the nearest wall. "Time to move on to the next tradition."

His fingers delved into her hair, fiddled with the tiara before removing it, leaving little prickles of hyper-awareness where his fingertips had brushed her scalp. Having him carry her, touch her, flirt with her, had been in good fun, but now, with a potent sexual attraction smoldering between them, it wasn't so funny.

"What's the next tradition?"

"The wedding night." His hands spanned her waist and lifted her slightly so she came in contact with evidence of how excited he was to consummate this marriage.

"But it's still morning."

His lips grazed her ear. "Good. Gives me a chance to see you better when I..."

She whimpered as he whispered in erotic detail what he wanted to do.

Right here. Right now.

She throbbed with anticipation, every inch of her straining toward him.

She wanted him to lick her and tease her and touch her until she came.

She wanted him to hoist her up against the wall and drive into her until she saw stars.

She wanted him to make her forget her own name. But a small part of her didn't want to set precedence. That this powerful guy could snap his fingers and get anything he wanted.

It wouldn't be good. She may have compromised her morals in marrying a guy she hardly knew and certainly didn't love. No way she would sell her soul for the sake of fabulous sex.

And it would be fabulous, she had no doubt. If the guy could kiss like that and turn her on to the extent she would willingly strip in broad daylight, the sex would be freaking sensational. Stupid thing was, she wasn't into one-night stands—she didn't like the cool, impersonal aspect—and that's exactly what sex with her new husband would be: frantic, quickie sex with a stranger.

If she slept with him, she wanted it to mean something. Corny, for a gal who didn't believe in romance or marriage, but she couldn't change now. She'd compromised enough by agreeing to his marriage terms—not too difficult, considering the five hundred grand.

His lips stilled against her neck. "What's wrong?"

"We should head back to Vegas. Get ready for the reception." Lame, but she knew how important it was to him to schmooze his investors and apparently they'd all be there, carefully assessing if the bad boy had made good.

"Screw the reception," he muttered, pulling away slowly.

Her body instantly regretted her holier-than-thou decision, clamoring for him to get up close and personal again. Thankfully, her head ruled. "You said it was important."

"It is." He braced his hands on either side of her head, effectively trapping her, and she couldn't fathom his tortured expression. Unless he was worried about the convincing performance she'd have to give.

"It's going to be okay." She placed her palm against his chest, directly over his pounding heart. "I can play the adoring wife, no probs."

"That's not what I'm worried about," he said, lowering his arms and thrusting his hands in his pockets.

"Then what's up?" He turned away, his back rigid, shoulders tense. "Beck?" She laid a tentative hand on his back and he spun around, his eyes dark.

"This thing between us. I don't want—I mean, I can't give you—"

She placed her fingertips against his lips, silencing him. "We're attracted to each other. No big deal."

He brushed away her fingers. "This marriage is strictly business. I don't want to take advantage of you, but..." He shook his head. "Fuck, I don't want to lose control."

"I can take care of myself." She'd done a good job of it so

far. Apartment in LA, thriving freelance marketing business, living the life.

So why did his sudden protective concern disarm her more than his kisses?

"I don't want anything from you, bar what we agreed on. I don't do emotions. I don't do complications." On impulse, she reached up and smoothed his lapel.

Surprisingly, he didn't swat her away. "What about a marriage with benefits?"

"Marriage with benefits," she echoed, as if trying it on for size and not liking the fit. She couldn't give in to him. She wouldn't. If only she could convince her traitorous body, which was practically straining toward him. Needing a quick change of subject, she said, "Why don't you give me the grand tour? Then we take our fake marriage duo act to your wedding shindig."

"What about those benefits?" He took a step toward her and she held him off with a fingernail to the chest. "We could get lucky."

She should've known he wouldn't accept her brushoff. "Doubtful," she said, giving him a gentle shove. Predictably, he didn't budge.

"Didn't you know?" He grabbed her hand and hauled her in close. "In Vegas everyone gets lucky."

"I thought the house always won."

"We're holding a stacked deck. We can't lose." His lips crushed hers, a swift, potent assault that left her gasping and yearning for more despite every self-preservation instinct screaming, "Invest in more granny panties now!"

She pushed him away, and this time he let her. "How magnanimous," she muttered, earning a grin as he snagged her hand and tugged her deeper into his house.

Correction: his *home*. That's what this place truly felt

like. Slate floors highlighting the rustic colors of the desert covered in a profusion of turquoise, butternut, and camel rugs. Low ochre suede sofas stacked with matching cushions, and surrounded by paintings depicting various Nevada backdrops, this place screamed cozy and comfy and liveable.

Which begged the question, why did he have it if he never spent any time here?

"It's gorgeous."

"I like it." He shot her a grateful glance, as if he'd expected her to criticize. "It's what I think a home should look like."

His flat intonation gave her a chill. Considering what he'd divulged about his family, she didn't blame him for wanting a house filled with warmth and color. All the more reason to hang out here.

"You should definitely come here more often." She said it offhand, carefully studying his reaction. Emotions may not have been part of their marriage deal, but it paid to get a heads-up on her business partner.

And that's all Beck was. She'd be foolish to think that just because he trusted her enough to bring her out here to his home, assuming he was showing her a part of himself he kept hidden, that it meant anything more.

She didn't want more. She wanted complication-free, so she could walk away without regrets once his deal was done.

"Business keeps me busy." He stared out the nearest window. "I travel a lot. Don't have time to sit back and smell the cacti."

She squeezed his hand. "This place is incredible. You should make time."

His prolonged silence unnerved her before he released

her hand and swung back to face her. "You're welcome to live here."

"While we're married, you mean?"

He nodded. "Make it easier on both of us, not having to keep up pretenses twenty-four-seven."

Damn, he was a hard one to read. One minute he was all over her, the next he wanted her as far away as possible. He was right, though. The less time they spent together the less chance of throttling each other, and she had no doubt they'd soon tire of playing happy newlyweds.

"Fine by me."

"Good. I'll show you the rest of the place."

And he did, taking her through the lavish bedrooms, the state of the art kitchen, the homey sunroom. But something had changed. He didn't hold her hand, and he described the place like a real estate agent: devoid of humor and emotion. When they stepped outside to the pool area, the blast of desert heat was a welcome relief from the chill inside: Beck was worse than the A/C.

He pointed at an outdoor kitchen. "Housekeeping comes in twice a week so the fridge will be stocked."

"Great." They stepped out from the shade of a veranda and strolled around the pool, an Olympic-sized oval surrounded by trimmed hedges and cacti in terracotta pots that matched the house's exterior.

"Cool place," she said, trying to look at the house with objectivity, but failing.

Both outside and in, it had character and charm and warmth, a real home.

That Beck deliberately kept empty.

"Will you be down here much while I'm staying?"

He stiffened, as if she'd asked him to streak through the desert at midday. "I'll have to spend some time at the house for appearances, but it's probably easier if you head to the Strip for functions I'll need you to attend."

"No problem." But she wouldn't give up that easily. Something about this place had him rattled, and if she was going to be stuck out here in hacienda heaven, she wanted to know what she'd be dealing with. "You should come down on weekends. Learn to chill out."

He fixed her with a disbelieving glare. "Don't try to change me because you've got a ring on your finger." He pointed to the diamond-studded platinum wedding band he'd slipped on less than an hour ago. "Those sparklers may be real, but everything else in this marriage is fake."

"Not everything," she muttered. A very real attraction simmered between them, and she earned another steely glare for her trouble.

"Come on, we've got a wedding reception to host."

"You're the boss." She saluted, another attempt at humor lost. He didn't break stride as he headed for the house, leaving her to ponder exactly what she'd gotten herself into with this inconvenient marriage.

∽

BECK SLAMMED his palm against a terracotta wall, barely registering the pain as he studiously avoided glancing outside at the cause of his discontent.

While Poppy investigated every nook of the desert garden, he mentally recited reasons why he shouldn't touch her.

Business deals should never be clouded with emotion.

Never mix business with pleasure.

Focus on signing the construction deal; avoid distractions.

Good, solid reasons. Closely followed by *all work and no play makes Beck a very dull—and frustrated—boy.*

He slipped a finger between his collar and neck, loosening it. Ever since he'd said, "I do," he hadn't been able to breathe, choked by his own foolishness. No matter how many times rationale dictated he keep his marriage to Poppy platonic, the simple fact was, he couldn't keep his hands off her.

Shit. She'd wisely given him time to cool off, but taking a prolonged dunk in the Hoover Dam wouldn't cool him. Nothing short of raunchy sex with his wife would do that. He'd thought hiding her away while he remained in Vegas would take the edge off. Establishing physical distance while utilizing the respectability his new marriage brought to seal the deal with the investors.

He'd screwed up. Every time he thought of her here he'd imagine her in his bed, his bath, his pool.

She'd be naked, of course. *Naked and willing...* He kicked a potted cactus, barely registering the sting of a stray spike.

The sooner he left his bogus wife here and headed back to Vegas, the better.

NINE

Divorce Diva Daily recommends:
Playlist: "Fool to Cry" by The Rolling Stones
Movie: War of the Roses
Cocktail: Bloody Mary

Beck preferred sleeping under the desert stars to the glittering pizzazz of a Vegas party, but this was one shindig he had to attend.

His wedding reception.

The staff had done a great job, turning the revolving rooftop dining room of his signature hotel into a gilt-edged wonderland filled with the best crystal, the best silver, and the best food money could buy. But as he sipped aged whiskey on the edge of a buzzing crowd, nothing about this evening seemed real.

As the sound of clinking crystal champagne flutes and muted laughter washed over him, he sucked in a breath that didn't ease the tightness in his chest.

He'd done the one thing he swore he'd never do. Get married. He didn't like codependence—on anything or anyone. He'd seen his mom develop both after she'd met his lousy dad. And Beck hated answering to anyone, but that's exactly what he'd had to do when he'd made the mistake of taking Poppy to the house. Even now, twelve hours later, he had no idea why he'd done it.

The moment she'd slipped the platinum band on his finger and he'd kissed his new bride, he'd wanted to get her alone. Naked.

And therein lay the problem. He'd already let her into his life by allowing her to stay at Red Rock Canyon, had already divulged too much in telling her all that stuff about his family history. Having her live in his home implied an intimacy he didn't want, and sex with her would solidify that.

It was more than that and he knew it. The house was the part of him he kept hidden from everyone else. None of his Vegas crowd had been there—not even Lou—and he liked it that way. He may have escaped Checkerville and his dreary past, but there was one thing he could thank his no-good folks for: helping to instil in him a love of the desert.

Pa had fostered his love for the arid landscape surrounding their trailer, had taken him on long hikes, pointing out the Joshua trees, the Mohave yucca, the Apache plume, while warning him of the dangers of scorpions, tarantulas, and Mohave green rattlers.

Beck had spent countless hours watching his favorite desert tortoise, coyote, and gila monster, chasing jackrabbits and studying roadrunner habits.

He loved the heat, the dust, the colors. Something Poppy had homed in on immediately. He'd seen the light in her eyes as she'd toured his home and it made him like her all the more. Which was why he'd shut down and put some serious emotional distance between them. He didn't want to feel anything for his wife, and that was a distinct possibility if they spent too much time together.

Poppy was nothing like the women he usually dated. She was warm and spontaneous and bold.

She didn't defer to him; she didn't play games. Hell, this marriage farce was testament to that. Poppy was blunt and genuine and far too appealing. The less time he spent with her, the better.

"There you are." She slipped her arms around his waist from behind and rested her cheek on his back, playing the doting wife for their reception guests. "Slipped off the ball and chain already?"

"I'm taking a breather." He turned around, secretly pleased when she didn't release him.

"Low stamina, huh?"

He ducked his head to whisper in her ear. "Wouldn't you like to know?"

"Not really." She laughed up at him, her eyes sparkling with mischief, and right then, snug in the circle of her arms, he'd never been more convinced he'd done the right thing in offering her the Red Rock Canyon house to stay in.

He thought he'd made a smart business move marrying this woman for convenience. But right now, enjoying the way she made him feel way too much? Dumb.

She stood on tiptoes to murmur in his ear. "Are we pulling this off?"

He sure as hell hoped so. Everyone had turned up: the investors, the work crew, a few A-listers. People he mingled with on a regular basis, people whose opinions shouldn't matter. But they did. He needed the investors to trust him, to trust Blackwood Enterprises enough to help take them national.

This marriage had to do that. It had to.

"We're doing okay."

"One thing's for certain, you sure know how to throw a party." Poppy released him to step back and take in the crowd. "But you know I'll top this for Lou's divorce party, right?"

"Shhh." He held a finger up to her lips, immediately regretting it when her eyes heated to molten chocolate and her lips parted on a soft sigh. "Don't say the D-word around here. People might question the validity of this marriage."

"You don't need to remind me about the importance of anonymity." The fire in her eyes faded. "Sara would have a coronary if she knew I was the divorce diva." She gestured at the crowd. "As for them questioning our marriage, people are going to do that anyway, considering how it happened out of the blue."

"Have you been interrogated by anyone?" Concern poked holes in his carefully constructed plan.

"Try everyone." She snorted. "Don't worry, I gave them the spiel we rehearsed. Your need for privacy, the long-distance thing, unable to be apart any longer."

"Did they buy it?"

Pensive, she glanced at the investors, a bunch of Scotch-swilling, backslapping suits that clung together like an old-boys club. "They seemed impressed, especially when I played up my Provost angle."

Some of the residual tension tightening his shoulders eased. "Thanks."

"Anytime." She kissed him on the cheek, a strangely sweet gesture that made his chest burn. "Better get back to mingling."

"Later." He snagged her hand and led her to the dance floor. "You were such a stickler for tradition with the threshold and all, it's only fair we have a bridal waltz."

Her smile faltered and for a mortifying moment he thought she'd bolt. He had no idea why dancing terrified her but with people already turning their way, they couldn't back out now.

"Two left feet, huh?"

"No, it's not that. It's…" She shook her head. "Nothing. Let's do this."

Beck nodded at the band, who struck up the song he'd specifically selected, U2's One. Appropriate. He wanted to be number one, wanted every person who'd ever laughed or scoffed or teased him in the past to know it.

Poppy stiffened in his arms as the lead singer did a great Bono impersonation, crooning about love being a temple and higher law, about one love, one life, one need in the night, the haunting lyrics effectively silencing the crowd. The hush was unnerving, but not as much as seeing the sheen of tears in Poppy's expressive eyes.

"You okay?" he mouthed.

She clearly wasn't, but she nodded, before burying her face in his chest.

His arms tightened around her waist and hers around his neck as they swayed together, their bodies in tantalizing contact, their souls a world apart. He didn't know what made his wife tick and for the first time since he'd devised this foolproof scheme, a sliver of remorse pricked his conscience. Maybe she wasn't as ballsy and blasé as she pretended to be. What if, God forbid, Poppy had bought into all this romantic wedding crap?

Yep, the sooner he packed her off to Red Rock Canyon, the better.

"You two make quite the couple." Stan Walkerville slapped Beck on the back and thrust a double malt into his hand.

Beck should've been ecstatic the head of the investors' conglomeration had sought him out. Instead, all he could think about was the way Poppy had reacted during that dance.

"Thanks." He raised his glass in Stan's direction. "Poppy's amazing."

"She sure is." Stan's beady stare followed Poppy as she slipped an arm through the crook of Ashlee's elbow and dragged her toward the dessert table.

Beck wanted to slug him.

"Comes from a good family, too. Parents are plastic surgeons, apparently."

"Yeah." Beck sipped his whiskey, taking the less-is-more approach. He'd memorized a whole bunch of facts about Poppy in case anyone quizzed him, but he didn't want to discuss her with Stan. He wanted to talk business. He couldn't be overt, though. Stan had to make the first move.

Discussing the nationwide deal at his wedding reception would raise flags.

"Good to see you settling down." Stan appraised him, his glare calculating, and Beck could imagine he was being sized up. "Good for your company, too."

Bingo. "Yeah, I'd been dragging the chain in our relationship. About time I made an honest woman out of her." He dredged up clichés, trying to make light of their discussion, when his heart pounded at the thought of getting another chance to make this deal happen.

"We should reconvene over that proposal of yours." Stan took a long slug of whiskey before slamming the glass down on a nearby table. "See if we can readjust the figures and make the deal happen."

"Definitely doable." If Beck sounded any more laidback he'd be horizontal, when all he wanted to do was punch the air and yell a resounding "Yes!"

"Set it up for end of next week." With one last leer in Poppy's direction that made Beck's fingers curl into fists, Stan nodded and walked away.

Beck should've been elated. He'd done it. Obtained the second chance he'd wanted, and this time he'd nail it.

Instead, as he watched Poppy fork a piece of key lime pie into her mouth and laugh at something Ashlee said, all he could think was the debt he owed her went beyond the money.

Way beyond. And he had no clue how to repay her.

∽

"DON'T LOOK NOW, but The Hottie is making goo eyes at you again." Ashlee elbowed Poppy, who risked a quick glance at Beck.

Ashlee was right. Even across the room, Poppy could see his slightly stunned expression.

Join the club. She'd been in shock ever since she set foot in this city and first laid eyes on him.

She waved at him, forcing the same bright, perky smile she'd used all evening, the one that said, "I'm a new bride and loving it." As opposed to the one she should've been sporting, the petrified grimace that said, "What the fuck am I doing?"

With a taciturn nod, he turned away and joined a group of suits and their stick-thin dates.

"That was weird." Ashlee bit into a vanilla custard profiterole, her blissful expression making Poppy smile.

"That's my husband," Poppy muttered, shoveling the last of her key lime pie into her mouth. She could've been eating cacti for all she cared, her favorite dessert barely registering as she mulled over what was going on in her husband's head.

"That's freaky."

"What?"

"You calling him your husband." Ashlee scooped the last of the custard from her plate and licked the spoon. "If I didn't know any better, I'd say you like it."

"You know why I'm doing this." Poppy lowered her voice and darted a look around to make sure no one else was within hearing distance.

"I know what you said at the start, but after today?" Ashlee cocked her head to one side, studying her. "I'm reassessing the situation."

Poppy knew what her BFF was implying. And she didn't like it. "Think what you like, you're talking out your—"

"Ass-essing, that's all I'm doing."

They laughed and Poppy sent a silent prayer heavenward in thanks that Ashlee knew the truth and she had someone to talk to. She would've gone nuts in this pretend marriage otherwise.

"Your husband sure knows how to par-tay."

Poppy had to agree. She loved the rooftop fairyland, complete with minuscule lights strung across the ceiling between billowing chiffon, ecru-covered chairs tied with gold bows, and the shimmer of crystal and silver everywhere. Every table had elongated rectangular vases filled with sparkly stone bases and long-stemmed blood-red roses as centerpieces. The name-tags were individually embossed gold on cream, and the exquisite food was laid out buffet style for people to help themselves.

Flame-grilled garlic oysters, pan-seared scallops, shrimp tempura, soy duck fillet, pork ribs in peppercorn sauce, poached fresh abalone, and wasabi beef fillet had kept the hordes fed, while the eight-piece band ensured the dance floor remained crowded…when they weren't jostling for position at the dessert bar for amaretto crème caramel, vanilla bean pannacotta, sticky mandarin pudding, nougat parfait, cappuccino cheesecake, and Poppy's favorite, key lime pie.

The overall effect was an elegant party, relaxed enough for revelers to enjoy themselves, classy enough to make them feel special.

Everyone except her. "Money can buy you anything."

"Including a wife, apparently."

Poppy knew Ashlee meant it as a joke, but the truth hurt. She had been bought. For a good cause, but bought nonetheless. And for a gal who hated rich folk flinging their money around to obtain anything, it irritated her. Hell, it bugged the crap out of her, but she owed Sara and finally, after all the years her sis had put into raising her, they were square.

"You're going to visit the office regularly, right?" Ashlee had the strained look of someone who'd only just realized what a monumental change had taken place and was trying to deal the best she could.

"Sure," Poppy said, knowing she'd miss her friend terribly, and frequent visits wouldn't help. "I need to see Sara once a week and I'll pop in then."

"It's a fair commute for weekly."

"I'll use the company jet. Beck won't mind." Especially

since he'd banished her to his desert hideaway. He wouldn't even notice she'd gone.

"Listen to you, Miss La-di-da." Ashlee mimicked drinking a cup of tea with her pinkie extended. "I'll just pop in on the company jet."

Poppy laughed at her fake posh accent. "There have to be some benefits to this crazy marriage."

Benefits... Which conjured up other potential benefits of being married to Beck, the kind that made her blood warm and her face flush.

"Apart from the obvious, you mean?" Ashlee snickered. "Try all you like, hon, but I see the way you two look at each other." She fanned her face with a napkin. "Scorching."

"There may be a little something there—"

"More like a whole hunk of burning love."

Poppy groaned and Ashlee said, "What? You think I'd come to Vegas and not make an Elvis wisecrack?"

"I'm going to miss you." Poppy slung an arm around her shoulder and hugged her.

"You won't have time, what with tending to your wifely duties."

"Just keep Party Hard afloat on your end and I'll do the rest from here." Poppy bumped her with her hip.

"The diva has spoken," Ashlee said, with a dramatic eye roll. "Let's see how long your divorce focus lasts when you're making out with The Hottie."

Poppy could've denied it, said she had no intention of making out with Beck, but she'd never lied to Ashlee and she wasn't about to start now.

It was all Poppy had been thinking about during the entire reception—not screwing up in front of his precious bloody investors—and how she'd keep him at arm's length once this party was over. For as much as they pretended the attraction between them didn't exist, it was there all the same: an underlying, potent simmer that grew exponentially the more she tried to deny it.

"I better get back to the guests."

"Poppy?"

"Yeah?"

"You're happy, right?" Ashlee had lost the goofy grin, a groove of concern crinkling her brows. "What you're doing for Sara? It goes above and beyond."

"I'm fine," Poppy said, but deep down she knew she wasn't.

Not since Beck had asked her to dance. She could cope with whatever this fake marriage dished up. But not the dancing. She should've told him before the reception to skip the bridal waltz. She hadn't, and she'd suffered the consequences.

Not that anyone except him had noticed how freaked out she'd been. The crowd had sighed, assuming she was so blinded by love she'd cried.

Beck wouldn't have made that assumption and she hoped he wouldn't ask her about it.

"Just so you know, I'm always a text or phone call away."

"Thanks, Ash." Who knew? Poppy might have to take Ashlee up on that offer before this marriage was through.

∼

WHEN THE LAST reveler had left, Poppy sagged in relief. "Boy, am I glad that's over."

"You and me both." Beck led her to the nearest chair and she sank gratefully onto it.

"How'd I do?"

He squatted in front of her and rested his forearms on her knees. A perfectly innocuous touch, but enough to send heat streaking up her legs. "You were magnificent."

"The bigwigs were impressed by your nuptial bliss?"

"Apparently so." His mouth twisted with a bitterness she didn't understand. "I've been asked to schedule another meeting to revisit the deal."

"That's great." In her excitement, she shifted, and his forearms slid off her knees, making him tumble.

"Trying to get rid of me already and the icing's barely set on the wedding cake?" He stood and dusted himself off, his wry grin endearing.

"Hardly." She tapped her bottom lip, pretending to ponder. "Besides, if I wanted to get rid of you I'd come up with more inventive ways."

"Such as?"

"You'll find out."

His grin faded. "You ever stop to think what the hell we're doing?"

Surprised at a rare display of doubt from the guy whose middle name had to be "Confidence," she shrugged. "We're smart people making decisions based on logic." She wrinkled her nose. "Not like the billion dummies out there who jump into situations feet first based on emotions."

"How'd you get so wise?" Admiration sparked his eyes as he sat beside her.

"Self-sufficiency breeds street smarts."

"Can't disagree with you there."

He looked like he wanted to ask questions, but she didn't want to answer any. This had been some day and now that she'd finally stopped moving, exhaustion blanketed her in a claustrophobic smother. She yawned.

"Time for bed?" Another unasked question hovered in

the silence between them as he studied her, waiting for her answer.

Heck, what was wrong with her? She never second-guessed herself for having sex with a hot guy. Not like this.

It was the damned ring snug on the third finger of her left hand that was causing all the problems.

For all the signed documentation and straight talk about this marriage being strictly business, she was starting to like Beck a tad. And that didn't bode well for an entanglement-free marriage.

"I'm going for a walk."

"Now?"

She nodded. "Need to clear my head."

"Marriage getting to you already?" He'd meant it as a joke but he'd pretty much homed in on what she was feeling, and she sprung up like a jack-in-the-box, eager to escape.

She'd known what she was getting into with this marriage, but after a long stressful day—heck, a long stressful week—it was tough facing reality. They'd gone into this marriage for purely mercenary reasons and it saddened her. She may not believe in marriage, but all the ones she knew of at least started with starry-eyed love.

Instead, she and Beck had reduced it to a cold, calculating business deal, and as she stared at the remnants of their red velvet wedding cake on its towering stand nearby, she had the distinct urge to sweep it onto the floor and trample it to crumbs.

He glanced at the cake and back at her, his expression wary. "I'll come with you."

"No."

He frowned. "What's wrong?"

She couldn't tell him the truth so she settled for the next

best thing. "I need some space." She gestured around the room. "All this pretending? Has taken it out of me. I need air."

He opened his mouth to respond and she held up a hand. "Alone."

"Okay." He sounded hurt and that hint of vulnerability from a tough guy like him had her softening the blow.

"I'm an independent person, Beck, always have been. So standing up in front of all these people and faking wedded bliss was an ordeal. I felt smothered and I need to get away."

"Is that why you freaked out during the bridal dance?"

What could she say? That dancing involved body contact, and she couldn't go there with him, not after his kisses. Uh-uh.

"Pretending sucks. I don't like the show we had to put on tonight for your buddies."

With a terse nod he turned away. She almost reached out to him. Almost. Her hand hovered halfway to his back before falling to her side. What was the point? This yawning gap between them was a good thing. Exactly what she wanted. No emotional involvement.

Then why the nagging unease that it may have been too late?

She slipped off her shoes, snagged them with her fingers, and ran for the elevator.

∽

BECK SWORE AFTER POPPY BOLTED.

He'd had grand plans for tonight. Plans that involved thanking his wife for the monumental role she'd played in helping him achieve what he wanted. A second chance with the investors.

Instead, he'd let her go. She'd been in a mood, part snit, part rebellion. It was like she'd wanted to pick a fight, but he wasn't biting. Sure, he understood her feeling stiffed. Tonight had been a mega ordeal for him, too, accepting backslaps and congratulations from people he'd known for years.

It was why the most important person in his life hadn't been here. He couldn't face lying to Pa and had taken the easy way out: called him when he knew his grandfather would be at the local stock car races and left a message. A lousy, vague excuse along the lines of "Hey, Pa, don't keel over, I've tied the knot. It would've been great for you to be here, but I'll explain when I get home. Soon."

Coward. Pa hated the cell phone and never used it. The only time they spoke was when Beck called him, far too infrequently these days. He knew he'd have to visit and tell Pa the truth in person.

Once he nailed the deal so it made his marriage sound halfway logical.

Pa understood practicalities. When Beck's folks had died, he'd stepped in and did what had to be done. Organized a makeshift room—a cleared space behind a tattered curtain—in his trailer, spoke to the teachers about his non-tolerance of truancy, and laid down the law to Beck in clear, concise terms.

He touched drugs, he was out on his own. Beck didn't have to be told twice. He had no intention of treading the same path as his loser parents. In fact, his memories of them drove him to excel, to ignore the taunts from the rich kids because he had holes in his sneakers or hand-me-down pants from the thrift shop.

He worked his ass off to get good grades, a scholarship to college, and a step into the life he craved. One where he didn't have to starve because he only had ten bucks in the bank and one where people looked at him with respect, not derision.

He owed Pa, and nothing less than the truth face-to-face would do. But first, he had to sort out the mess with his wife.

His wife. It sounded ludicrous, but he'd married Poppy to achieve a goal, and with that goal in sight he wanted to reassure her he would keep his end of the bargain. Sure, it'd be tough keeping up appearances for a while, but getting her offside on their wedding day didn't bode well for the rest of the marriage, fake or not.

Thankful he'd had the latest elevator technology installed in his hotel, he burst out of the entrance two minutes later. The Strip teemed with life. Goggle-eyed tourists rubbernecking, young guys cruising, local casino employees hurrying to work.

He loved the desert but there was something about this city that made his blood fizz.

He stepped onto the pavement and inhaled, car fumes and designer perfume and dust clogging his nostrils. People jostled him and the bright lights cast a permanent dawn in the sky. Rap music from a passing limo clashed with car horns and the blend of foreign accents from all around.

Yeah, the cosmopolitan buzz had him hooked. He'd traveled extensively for business but whenever he glimpsed the Grand Canyon out of the plane window, he knew he was almost home.

A home that was doing a damn fine job of hiding his wife.

He edged through the crowd, striding through the gaps,

scanning ahead. Luckily he only hired the best, and his concierge had pointed which way she'd gone.

The Blackwood, nestled between the Monte Carlo and the Mandarin, was in the heart of prime Strip hotels. Unable to stop a habit of a lifetime, something he'd developed as a young kid the first time his folks brought him here, he mentally recited hotel names.

Aria and Vdara on his left before he hit Harmon, Paris, and Bally's on his right after it.

Memorizing and reciting names had been fun as a kid. Now it served to annoy the hell out of him, as every hotel he passed made him wonder if Poppy had gone into any of them and given him the slip. His heart sank as he passed the Cosmopolitan and Bellagio on his left, crossed Flamingo Ave, and hit Caesar's Palace.

She couldn't have got this far so fast, not in those sky-high heels. Before he belatedly realized she'd taken them off before she left.

Dammit, he'd lost her. Failure didn't sit well with him, never had, and he clenched his fists, wishing he could punch something.

That was when he caught sight of her, way ahead, halfway between Mirage and Treasure Island. She was moving fast, practically jogging, and he broke into a sprint.

What the hell was she doing? She'd break her neck even without those heels.

Those heels…the moment he'd caught sight of her in them strolling toward him for their ceremony, he'd pictured her wearing them and little else.

Major turn-on, naked Poppy in poppy stilettos.

Okay, so fantasizing wasn't the smartest move, considering his hard-on seriously hampered his land speed record.

Cursing under his breath, he ran, apologizing to pedestrians he edged around, gaining ground.

As he closed the distance between them, he put on an extra burst of speed. Even from a distance she looked magnificent, five-five of defiant diva in a satin wedding dress. Another thing he liked about this town: its tolerance and open-mindedness. No one batted an eyelid at the babe in a wedding dress strolling down the Strip with her stilettos dangling from her fingers.

She paused at Treasure Island and he strode faster, beyond relieved when he finally reached her. Leaning casually alongside her, he waited until his breath steadied. "You have a thing for pirates, huh?"

"What the hell are you doing here?" She whirled to face him, indignation sparking her eyes caramel.

"I didn't want you walking out here alone." The simplicity of the truth struck him, as did his sudden protectiveness.

Her eyes narrowed, not diminishing their rampant distrust one iota. "I'm a big girl. I'm used to taking care of myself."

"I understand the independence thing. I'm the same way."

She crossed her arms, the simple action pushing her breasts together and creating eye-catching cleavage over the top of her strapless dress. "Yeah, you value your independence so much you couldn't wait for the ink to dry on the marriage certificate before exiling me to the desert."

Is that what this snit was about? A living arrangement that suited them both?

"I'm not shipping you off. We're both used to being on our own. I thought you'd appreciate the freedom to do your own thing—"

"While you do the same here?" She took a step closer and he stuck his hands in his pockets to stop from reaching for her. "It seemed to slip our minds, what with organizing a quickie wedding, but shouldn't we discuss whether this sham is monogamous? Because I won't tolerate being the talk of the town as Beck Bloody Blackwood screws around while poor wifey is stuck in the desert."

He recoiled as if she'd struck him. "Is that what you think of me?"

"I don't know you." She ended on a hitch and turned away but not before he glimpsed sadness pinching her mouth.

Hell, none of this was turning out as he imagined. Sure, the logistics of the wedding had gone smoothly, but the emotional side of things? Far more complicated than he'd anticipated. He didn't want to make her sad. He wanted to make tonight special to thank her for giving him the opportunity to make his corporate dreams a reality.

"When I make a promise I keep it, and that includes our wedding vows."

She continued to stare at the pirate ship, her spine rigid, her profile stoic.

"I didn't think you'd need me to spell it out, but here goes. We don't sleep around on each other for the duration of the marriage. Deal?"

She grunted in response.

"Besides, that's not the reason I offered you the house." He had to do something to save this disastrous evening and it looked like only the truth would do.

She must've caught the sincerity in his tone because she half turned, studying him with wary interest. "Then why?"

"Because I can't keep my hands off you," he blurted, encouraged by her wide-eyed surprise. "You distract me, and I can't afford distractions, not while this deal hangs in the balance. So it's easier to not have you around, tempting me to..."

"What?"

He could've sworn the air between them crackled as he debated telling her all of it. He'd come this far. If he wanted to change the outcome of tonight, now was the time to go the whole way. "To lose control."

He dragged a hand through his hair, more rattled now than the first time he stumbled on his folks spaced out in the backyard. "You're driving me crazy. You're all I can think about. Work used to consume me. I'm always in control there. But you—" He grabbed her upper arms, hauled her close. "You're making me lose it and I'm freaking out."

She eyeballed him, direct, unflinching, so he saw the moment she shifted from belligerent to appreciative. "You want me, huh?"

"What do you think?" He pulled her in closer still, leaving her in little doubt how much.

"Well, too damn bad." She tried to push him away but he didn't budge, liking having her close way too much to be good for him. "You can't have it both ways, hotshot."

"Wanna make a bet?" His best smile had little effect, if the frown between her brows was any indication.

"Not interested in gambling."

"Yet you gambled on me?"

"Correction: you left me no choice but to marry you, remember?"

His conscience pricked for a second, until he remembered Stan giving him another chance at the reception and his guilt eased. "What's a little blackmail between friends?"

"Friends?" She snorted and tried shoving him away again. "We were never friends."

"How about taking a shot at lovers, then."

She shook her head. "You don't quit, do you?"

"Not in my vocab." His hands splayed across the small of her back and he watched her eyes widen and the tip of her tongue dart out to moisten her lower lip. He wasn't imagining the flare of heat in her gaze or the involuntary arch toward him as his hand drifted lower to caress her butt.

"So you think you can banish me to the desert, but I'll jump into bed with you when it's convenient?"

He winced at her blunt assessment of the situation. "I think we'll be happier living apart, and yeah, I want you." He tried another coaxing smile. "We may have a fake marriage, but how about we go have ourselves a real wedding night to remember?"

"I hate you," she muttered, indecision pinching the corners of her lush mouth. "But I have to give you points for being up front about what you want."

"What do you want?" She hesitated an eternity, gnawing on her bottom lip, before her challenging gaze met his.

"You."

TEN

Divorce Diva Daily recommends:
Playlist: "Poker Face" by Lady Ga-Ga
Movie: Waiting to Exhale
Cocktail: Avalanche

Beck liked no-fuss.

He dated, he had sex. Complication free. But as he stepped into the bedroom of his penthouse suite with Poppy wedged against his side and watched her face flush with pleasure at the sight of the bed, he had the distinct feeling he'd initiated one big complication waiting to happen.

"You did this?" She slipped out from under his arm and padded toward the bed.

"Yeah."

Her fingertips trailed through the hundreds of poppies strewn across the black satin coverlet.

His gut clenched. Was the gesture too corny? Too overt? Too much?

She picked up a delicate flower and lifted it to her nose, closing her eyes as she inhaled. A slow, sweet smile tilted her mouth as she brushed the petals across her cheek and opened her eyes, fixing him with a seductive stare that socked him like a knockout punch he'd once experienced in the schoolyard. "Considering your obvious obsession with all things poppy, I'm starting to doubt your masculinity."

He relaxed at her playful tone and stalked toward her. "You won't be saying that come morning."

She laughed, a simple joyous sound that made him want to hold her all night long, and reinforced what he already knew deep down. Sleeping with her would guarantee complications with a capital C.

"Confident much?"

"You tell me." He backed her up a few inches until her knees hit the bed and she fell backward.

"I'll have to see what you've got first," she said, radiant in a sea of poppies, her arms stretched overhead, elevating her dress to X-rated proportions as it revealed a tempting expanse of thigh.

His heart jack-knifed. She was beyond sexy. And she was all his. "Sure you're ready for it?"

"Oh, I'm ready." She picked up a handful of poppies and tossed them in his face, chuckling like she knew some great secret he didn't.

"Think you're a tough girl, huh?"

"I don't think, I know."

Picking poppies out of his hair, her fingertips skimmed his scalp, making it prickle. She arched, bringing her body in temptingly close contact with his in an overt invitation. "The question is, can you handle me?"

He didn't need to be asked twice. "I can handle anything you dish out and more, sweetheart."

He skimmed his hand down her body, starting at her cleavage and moving lower. The satin of her dress felt slippery beneath his palm, until he realized he was probably sweating.

Him, nervous? Never. He reached just below her navel when his wedding ring snagged on a crystal and she chuckled. "I don't usually get laughed at in the bedroom."

"Why not? Sex is fun." She winked. "Unless you're into that painful kinky stuff—"

"You talk too much." He yanked his hand free and covered her mouth with his. Deepened the kiss. His tongue entwining with hers in a long, hot, mind-numbing kiss that assured him this was right.

They were both panting when they came up for air. And grinning.

Bizarre. He'd never had fun sex before. He liked it.

"Careful. Looks like you're enjoying yourself." She traced his bottom lip with her fingertip, a slow sensual sweep that intensified the anticipation.

"And we haven't even got to the good part yet." Her fingertip left his mouth, trailed along his jaw, his chest.

Lower.

She toyed with the waistband of his trousers, fiddled with the belt buckle, and he gritted his teeth at the exquisite torture. When she cupped his erection, he groaned.

She squeezed. "This the good stuff you were referring to?"

"And the rest." He growled as he lowered himself flush against her, nuzzling her neck, nipping gently. She writhed beneath him, her soft moans firing his libido. Like it needed that. His body roared for her.

He'd had grand plans to seduce her slowly, to prolong the pleasure. Those plans were shot the moment she'd touched him. He needed more. He needed all of her. Now.

"I want you."

Her lips stilled the exploration of his neck. She captured his face in her hands and looked him straight in the eye. "Right back at you."

She surged upward, plastering her mouth to his, her hands desperate as they plucked at his dress shirt. Unable to find purchase, she slid her fingers between the cotton and ripped, the buttons pinging onto the wooden floorboards.

Flowers flew as their frantic hands made quick work of their clothes. She pushed his shirt off his shoulders, kissing her way across his collarbone. He unzipped her dress and she shimmied out of it, leaving her in a cream satin strapless bra and matching thong covered in tiny red poppies. What else?

"Snap." He picked up one of the poppies off the bed and brushed it over one breast, covering her right nipple.

She moaned and came up into a kneeling position. "Great minds think alike."

He unhooked her bra as she slid his belt free. He hooked his thumbs under the elastic of her thong and wiggled it down as she eased his boxers over his straining erection.

He gritted his teeth when she enclosed him in her fist. And pulled. Gently.

His head fell back on a groan as she increased the pressure. Blindly, he reached out, zeroing on her slick heat, circling her clit.

"Oooh..." Her appreciative murmur fired his blood and before things escalated too far, too fast, he stilled her hand and managed to flip her onto her back in a smooth move that left her gasping.

"Talented and acrobatic. I like," she said, staring up at him from beneath lowered lashes.

"If that impressed you, wait until you see what's coming up." He knelt on the floor, slid his hands behind her knees, and tugged her toward him. He splayed her legs, opening her to him. He tongued her, savoring her small sighs and soft yelps as he eased a finger into her wetness.

It nearly killed him, taking it slow, but she was so responsive, so beautiful. When her hands delved into his hair and held him to her, only then did he pick up the pace, and she shattered on the third swirl of his tongue, screaming his name.

Then she raised her head. Their gazes locked. And he experienced something he'd never had in all his past sexual encounters.

A connection. A connection that went beyond the physical, the type of unspoken link that needed no words yet spoke volumes.

A connection that scared the shit out of him.

This had to be about sex. It had to. He couldn't handle getting emotionally involved. It wouldn't end well.

"You were right. You're beyond talented."

"You ain't seen nothing yet."

Eager to dispel the intimacy that could prove to be his undoing, he snagged his wallet out of his pants and slipped a condom out. He sheathed himself in record time, eager to be inside her, desperate to lose himself in the physical and obliterate any semblance of intimacy.

She opened her arms to him and he rejoined her on the bed, entering her in one swift thrust that made her cry out in pleasure.

Heaven. Tight, slick, heaven. Surrounding him. Clenching him.

He'd wanted to prolong this. Not now. Later. And then she started moving beneath him, lifting her legs to lock around his waist, taking him in deeper.

That's when he lost it. He drove into her like a man possessed, loving how she met him thrust for thrust.

His abs cramped with the force of it and as the blood roared in his ears and his brain effectively blanked, she bit into his shoulder.

He came in a cataclysmic explosion that shook him to his core, unable to think, unable to register anything beyond... *fuck.*

What they'd just done? Had blown his mind.

He'd just had the best sex of his life.

With his wife.

∼

POPPY LIKED DATING and she enjoyed sex, but she'd never been a fan of the one-night stand.

Which made her decidedly grumpy when she woke the next morning to find her husband gone and a crappy note propped on the bedside table.

Thanks for yesterday.

Duty calls. In meetings all day.

Red Rock Canyon departure changed. Need to attend several functions before you leave in a few days.

Beck.

She stared at the note in disbelief before crumpling it and flinging it halfway across the room.

Arrogant, smug bastard. *Thanks for yesterday.* What was that? Forced, polite appreciation for marrying his conceited hide? Or for the most amazing, wanton night of her life?

And way to go with organizing when her departure would occur and lack of a sign-off. No "Love." No xx.

She could wring his neck.

She paced the monstrous bedroom, scuffing wilted poppies along the way. Kicking the flowers didn't make her feel a whole lot better, but it did succeed in working off some of her anger. By the time she'd made her sixth circuit of the room, she felt calm enough to take a good look around.

Ebony carpets. Chrome-edged furniture. High-tech blackout blinds. While its modernity was appealing, the starkness of the bedroom reinforced what she already knew. Beck Blackwood didn't do fuss. He didn't like clutter or stuff. He liked orderly and precise and well controlled—as long as he was doing the controlling.

Even last night had been about control. He'd planned the seduction; the poppies were evidence of that. He'd pleasured her repeatedly with his hands and mouth—not that she could complain—but hadn't given her time to return the favor, taking her every which way, inventing positions she hazarded to guess the Kama Sutra hadn't depicted yet.

Exiling her to Red Rock Canyon? Yeah, further signs of a control freak.

She wanted to rebel. She wanted to barge into his office, lay across his desk, and dare him to deny what they both felt last night. Very real proof that this marriage went beyond convenient.

A second after the thought registered in her sleep-deprived brain, she fell back on the bed and pulled the covers over her head.

What was she thinking? She didn't want to acknowledge there was anything in this marriage beyond money.

And sex, thanks to how she'd foolishly given in to him last night. Thinking along the lines of more…nope, crazy.

Being banished to the desert after his precious bloody functions was a good thing. She'd have loads of time to plan Lou's divorce party and do some online marketing for Divorce Diva Daily. With the bonus of getting some distance and perspective between her and him. Yeah, that's exactly what she'd do. Beck Blackwood could go about his business and she'd go about hers.

Far away from mesmerizing green eyes and sexy stubble and a mouth made for sin.

∽

BECK HAD PLANNED on taking a twenty-four hour vacation the day after his wedding. People would expect it, would think he'd be holed up in his penthouse with his new wife.

That had been the plan. Until last night. Last night had changed everything.

He was no longer under any illusions that marriage to Poppy would be a simple business affair. She had something about her, something with the capacity to reach down to his soul and tweak, hard. He didn't let anyone get close, least of all a woman who was mercenary enough to marry for money. Never mind that he was being harsh in judging her, considering he'd left her little choice in the matter. In fact, he respected her for doing what she did to save her sister's business. Not many women would go to those lengths, marry a virtual stranger, for family.

But he couldn't afford to admire her. Admiration led to liking, and liking led to…genuine feelings.

And last night he'd come pretty close to doing just that.

Feeling. The foreign sensation had driven him straight to the office this morning, scuttling his plans for a leisurely breakfast in bed followed by a day of decadent sex.

He couldn't afford to lounge around with Poppy all day, being cozy and intimate. Who knew what the outcome would be? No, it was much safer keeping his distance, interacting at the obligatory functions that had landed in his inbox late last night, and then bundling her off to Red Rock Canyon while he concentrated on nailing this deal.

Only one problem. Despite working his ass off for the last three hours, setting up another meeting with Stan Walkerville's PA, going over his last pitch and refining it, ensuring he'd dotted his Is and crossed his Ts, he couldn't stop thinking about her.

She invaded his thoughts constantly. The tilt of her lips when she touched him. The tiny sigh of wonder she made when he entered her. The sheen of perspiration highlighting her post-coital glow.

It was all he could think about. The pen he was holding skewed off the page and ripped a hole in it, and he threw it on the desk in disgust. He couldn't afford distractions. Not now, when he was one step closer to achieving the ultimate goal. So what the hell was he going to do about shutting his wife out of his mind?

The door edged open and Lou stuck his head around it. "Got a minute?"

"Yeah." Wasn't like he'd get any more work done now he'd allowed himself to fantasize about Poppy for more than a few seconds. "Come in."

Lou strolled into the office, shoulders squared, hands in pockets, looking a hundred times better than he had the last month.

"What's up with you?"

"Got an email from that party planner." Lou pulled his smartphone out of his pocket and brandished it. "She sent some epic ideas through for my divorce party."

"Good." That's all he needed, another reminder of his wife.

"But that's not why I'm here."

"Let me guess. You've finished compiling the hotel profit margins and want to dazzle me?"

"You know we're making a killing." Lou slid into the seat on the other side of his desk. "I'm not here to talk work."

"Oh?"

"You and Poppy." Lou crossed his fingers. "Like that."

"And your point?"

"How come you never mentioned her? Especially that night I was blind and raving on about you finding a quickie wife." Lou puffed out his chest. "I'm your best bud."

"Since when have we traded girlie stories?"

"Pre-Julie days, a long frigging time ago." Lou slumped in his chair.

"Exactly. You haven't exactly been with it since the separation and I've been working my ass off trying to seal the nationwide deal. Not much time left for…" Beck lifted an imaginary whiskey glass to his mouth. "We've had different priorities. You've been getting over Julie, I've been handling work and a long-distance relationship."

Beck hated lying to Lou, one of the few people in this world he could trust, but Lou was a loose cannon at the moment. His reliable bud had been drunk too often for his liking since Julie left, and while it hadn't affected his work, Beck had seen how alcohol loosened lips. And he had no intention of Lou inadvertently sinking his ship before it had sailed.

"You still could've told me." Lou frowned. "Especially when she has super powers."

"Huh?"

"Any woman who can get you to the altar, let alone slip a ring on your finger, must have mystical powers."

"Poppy's special." Beck shrugged, trying to act casual as his chest twanged, an instant reminder that maybe his aim to deceive Lou held a grain of truth. She was special. He'd known it from the moment she'd stood up to him and refused his offer.

As for last night...great, there he went again, focusing on the incredible sex.

"You're a lucky son of a bitch," Lou said, gesturing around the room. "I used to envy you all this, but now? You've got it all." He stood and pointed to the documents strewn across his desk. "Take it from me, man. If I were you, I wouldn't be stuck here the day after my wedding. I'd be home paying attention to the missus."

Beck only just caught his muttered, "Something I should've done more often," as Lou headed out the door.

The last thing Beck wanted to do was pay more attention to Poppy. But as he blindly stared at the spreadsheets, with the lies he'd told his best bud echoing through his head, all he could think was, *Who was he really lying to?*

ELEVEN

Divorce Diva Daily recommends:
Playlist: "Hit Me with Your Best Shot" by Pat Benatar
Movie: One Fine Day
Cocktail: Angel's Lips

Poppy had just zipped her overnight bag when Beck barged into the penthouse suite.

"Change of plans. We need to attend one last party before you head out to the desert."

Poppy hated being told what to do almost as much as having to jump to his tune because she'd agreed to this farce of a marriage. That didn't mean she'd make it easy for him. "Is that right?"

"Don't give me grief." He shrugged out of his jacket and ripped off his tie before heading for the bathroom. "I'm not in the mood."

"Not what you said last night." If her barb registered he didn't show it as he splashed water on his face, spritzed aftershave, and grabbed a fresh tie from his extensive collection.

Cheap shot, considering she was as much to blame for the last few nights' lapse as he was, but the fact he ignored her during the days following sizzling nights really rankled. It shouldn't. Not with a clear-cut business agreement of a marriage. But it did. Sue her for being a fickle female prone to flights of fantasy: like the one where he'd rush into the penthouse and rip off her clothes because he'd been as stunned by their connection the last three nights as she was.

"We need to put in an appearance at a party thrown by one of the investors. Shouldn't take more than an hour or two." He swapped cufflinks and plucked a new jacket out of the closet, not looking at her the entire time.

"Beck?"

"Yeah?"

"You may have blackmailed me into marrying you, but I'm not some puppet you can jerk around who'll perform on cue."

His head snapped up, his gaze accusatory. "That's not what I'm doing."

"Like hell it isn't." She marched across the penthouse and into his personal space. When his crisp aftershave tickled her nose, she stepped back, scared by the intense impulse to nuzzle his neck and inhale. "Your type likes calling the shots, I get it. But a little courtesy doesn't go astray, so next time, text or call me."

If she'd expected him to appear suitably chastised, she was sorely disappointed.

"My type?"

"Bigshot. Used to getting his own way, expecting subordinates to jump."

His eyes narrowed to green sabers. "That's not how I treat you—"

"Yeah, it is." She whirled away, surprised by the flicker of hurt cramping his mouth. "You want this marriage to be a business arrangement, fine, but start treating me with the same respect you'd afford your colleagues."

He whistled low. "You don't pull any punches."

"Stop acting like an arrogant jerk."

He laid a hand on her shoulder and she jumped, so consumed by her fury she hadn't heard him sneak up behind her. "I'm sorry."

She heard true contrition and her anger fizzled. They didn't have a real relationship so she shouldn't care this damn much. Powerful guys in her past wouldn't apologize if she begged, so for Beck to capitulate so quickly earned her respect.

"You're forgiven," she said begrudgingly as she turned to face him, unprepared for the uncertainty clouding his face.

"Let's put in an obligatory appearance at this party so I can head—" she almost said home, but quickly amended to "—out to the desert."

Everything about this arrangement was temporary, so why did she feel so blah about shacking up at Red Rock Canyon for the interim, until his precious deal went through? Already requests for quotes were flooding into the Divorce Diva Daily site, and between that and corresponding with Ashlee about Party Hard's plans in the works, she hadn't had time to breathe the last few days.

There was plenty to keep her busy between putting in obligatory appearances at Beck's functions. He'd asked her to stick around for three days to show a united front to the doubters and she'd done it. More fool her, because all she'd succeeded in doing was feeding an addiction...to her new husband.

"Thanks for being a good sport about all this. I appreciate it," he said, his gruffness belied by a soft kiss on her cheek.

She mumbled a response and fell into step beside him as they headed downstairs for the latest meet-and-greet. They didn't touch until they neared the function room, when he snagged her hand. All for show, of course, and she tried to ignore the niggle of regret that wormed its way through her pragmatic acceptance of the situation.

She hated pretending for his cronies, hated how she felt when he wasn't around more: irrationally missing him a tad. How could she miss someone she barely knew? Someone she'd spent a few freaking nights with? Crazy.

But she couldn't help it, and every morning when she woke to find his side of the bed empty, she'd remember the night before and how he'd made her feel.

Like the most beautiful woman in the world. Beck was the type of guy to get under a girl's skin and that was exactly what he'd done. She admired his ruthlessness in doing whatever it took to get the job done, including marrying. Not many people would go to such lengths. Ironically, he was probably thinking the same about her. If he knew Sara and saw how much she'd deteriorated since her marriage imploded, he'd understand.

Which made it all the more imperative she kept Divorce Diva Daily under wraps.

"WILL any of these people be at Lou's party?" Beck nodded and gripped her hand tighter as they eased into the room.

"You've seen the guest list. Lou's inviting every occupant of the state of Nevada and half of California, too."

"I should play nice, then?" Considering the A-listers Lou had insisted she invite, if she nailed his party she'd virtually secure Sara's future beyond Beck's cash injection.

Business would boom and in time, when Sara was stronger and less vulnerable emotionally, Poppy could tell her the truth and present her with a thriving business she'd be foolish to shut down. Yeah, she had it all figured out. Except the part where her heart beat faster every time her husband glanced her way.

"Playing nice for this crowd is the only way you'll escape unscathed."

She didn't understand his bitterness or the frown he quickly erased when she glanced at him. She had her own reasons for hating glitzy parties like this: she'd grown up with them, had despised every fake schmoozing minute. But guys like Beck moved in these moneyed circles all the time, thrived with the backslapping and BS.

So why did he look like he'd rather be anywhere but here?

"Shouldn't you mingle?" She gave him a gentle bump with her hip but he didn't budge, her hand way too comfortable in his.

"It's all about being seen and we're doing that." His stony gaze swept the crowd. "I'm so over this," he muttered, pinching the bridge of his nose with his free hand.

"I thought you loved the schmoozing."

"You would think that," he said, releasing her hand. "Drink?"

"Champagne, please."

His brusque nod made her heart sink. She could think the worst of her blackmailing husband, but why couldn't she keep her big mouth shut and not articulate it every five seconds? She watched him thread his way through the crowd, being stopped every few feet to air-kiss a fake-tanned bimbo or shake hands with pretentious jackasses.

Rather than thriving under the attention, she saw him slip a finger between his tie and too-tight collar, glance at his watch three times, and cut short conversations with a brittle grin.

But the real surprise occurred when he neared the bar. One of his underlings she'd met in passing was juggling a cell in one hand and an iPad in the other, appearing stressed and frenetic simultaneously. Beck stopped, relieved the guy of the iPad, and started typing while the guy straightened like a weight had been lifted off his shoulders, talking into his cell while dictating something to Beck.

Fascinated, Poppy watched Beck smile and nod at the guy as they worked together, completely at ease in a way he hadn't been with the rest of the crowd of his contemporaries. And at that moment, she realized she'd misjudged him. He wasn't like the rich jerks in her past. He valued hard work and commitment, and tolerated the rest of the trappings for appearance's sake.

All the fake schmoozing? Something he did for his business, not something he enjoyed. She already knew how far he'd go for his business—marrying her was proof enough—but seeing him treat his underling as an equal went a long way to making her appreciate him in a new light. She didn't want him to unveil a softer side, would rather hate him for blackmailing her into this situation than like him. But what she'd just seen could have pushed her a little past the like stage—and that freaking terrified her more than all the Gila monsters in the desert.

THE MOMENT BECK caught sight of Poppy lounging in the sun, incredibly tempting in an emerald string bikini held together by willpower alone, he knew he shouldn't have come.

One problem. He couldn't stay away. He'd tried—hell, he'd tried. For four days straight. He'd buried himself in work, getting up at five, working out for an hour—it did little for the sexual frustration making him edgy and moody and downright dangerous to be around—then hitting his desk and working until midnight.

It didn't help. He'd gone over every document for his meeting with Stan on Friday ten times, ensuring his proposal was rock solid. Besides, he had a feeling this meeting was a formality. Stan already knew what Blackwood Enterprises was capable of. He just hadn't trusted their reputation.

Which now, thanks to the stunning woman lying in the sun like some ancient goddess, had solidified in the eyes of the old-school investor. It irked Beck, not being trusted, especially when he'd put in the hard work to make this company the best in the business. But he, more than anybody, knew people only saw what they wanted to see.

Kids in high school hadn't seen his eagerness to fit in or his propensity for figures. They'd seen a scruffy kid in hand-me-down clothes with second-hand textbooks who lived in a trailer, and they'd treated him accordingly. If there was one thing he couldn't stand it was condescension, and it had driven him every day through high school and beyond.

Sad thing was, those same people sucked up to him whenever he visited Pa. And he pitied them. He'd once thought he'd lord it over those who had made his life in

Checkerville a misery, but a small part of him felt sorry for them.

Their lives were reduced to a fishbowl where their kids continued the bullying cycle, while he'd moved so far beyond all that it wasn't funny. The fact that Pa now lived in a ranch-style house he'd always dreamed of, with a garage full of vintage cars he loved, was vindication enough he'd done good.

Poppy shifted in her sleep, half turning onto her side, effectively pushing her breasts together with one half spilling out of its cup. His groin tightened and he gritted his teeth against the urge to barge over there and ravish her on the spot.

She looked delectable, a dorky white straw hat shading her face, her hair tumbling around her shoulders, her lips parted as she breathed deeply. She'd acquired a deeper tan since being out here, glorious expanses of golden skin on display just begging to be touched... He couldn't wait any longer. Skirting the pool, he strode toward her, certain his footsteps against the flagstones would wake her.

It didn't.

Even with his shadow looming over her she didn't stir, so he bent down and brushed a soft kiss against her lips.

Her eyelids snapped open and before he could react, she'd leapt up and simultaneously shoved him.

Beck teetered on the edge of the pool for a second, long enough to see the dawning horror spread across her face before he toppled backward. He fell in, submerged, grateful for solar heating. Not so grateful he was wearing an Armani suit and a Rolex.

He surged toward the surface in time to see her hovering on the edge of the pool, concern twisting her mouth into a grimace.

"Nice day for a swim." He frowned.

She winced. "Sorry, I thought you were some sicko sneaking into the backyard."

"That's what the alarmed walls are for, if you turned them on." As he tread water, a glimmer of an idea shimmering into his subconscious. A very naughty idea. "You were pretty out of it."

"Working hard." She jerked a thumb at her laptop. "What are you doing here?"

"Didn't want my wife pining away for me."

"As if." She towered over him, hands on hips, utterly delectable.

"Go on, admit it."

"What?"

"You missed me." She blew him a raspberry in response. "Your ego's as big as your fortune."

"I was hoping you'd say as big as something else."

A hint of a smile tugged at her mouth. "You've got a filthy mind, too."

"It's a guy thing." He swam closer, her dainty ankle within tempting reach.

Something in his expression must've alerted her to his nefarious intentions, because she edged back a little. "I'm putting the finishing touches on Lou's party. Why don't you dry off and we'll catch up later?"

"Why don't we catch up now?" Before she could move, his hand snaked out, grabbed her ankle, and tugged. She shouted an obscenity—several in fact—as she toppled into the pool beside him. Her hat floated to the surface a second before she did, sputtering and coughing.

"You play dirty." She shoved him away as he reached for her, and he laughed.

"You love it."

"Smug bastard," she muttered, her glare softening when his hands spanned her waist and tugged her closer.

"I love it when you call me names." He claimed her mouth before she could respond, the latent heat between them igniting in a fiery instant. His hard-on twitched as she wrapped her legs around his waist, bringing her in tantalizingly close contact.

She kissed him like she'd missed him and the feeling was entirely mutual.

Heading for the shallows, he waited until his feet found the bottom before backing her up against the side of the pool. They came up for air, gasping, her wide-eyed gaze mirroring his terror at how damned good they were together.

"We should get you out of those wet clothes," she said, her hands already pushing his jacket off his shoulders.

"Later." He released her long enough to unzip his pants and fish a soggy wallet out of his back pocket.

"Lucky foil's waterproof," she said, her decadent smile making his fingers fumble. "Let me."

While he shrugged out of his sodden jacket, kicked off his shoes, and wriggled out of his pants, her fingers slid off the slippery foil several times before finally ripping. When she reached for him, he was ready to plunge into her, protection be damned. Yeah, he was that crazily out of control.

He almost came when she touched the head of his penis and he couldn't watch as she unrolled the condom along his shaft with deliberate slowness. The second she was done, he tugged off her bikini, hoisted her up and slid into her on a loud groan.

She propped her arms behind her on the top step, opening herself to him beneath the scorching sun. Water droplets clung to her skin, and as he drove into her repeatedly he watched them run in tempting rivulets between her bouncing breasts.

He touched her clit, circling it with his thumb, varying the pressure until she fell apart on a yell, and he joined her a second later, shooting into her with a cataclysmic climax that blew his mind.

It took at least ten seconds for rational thought to return, and when he summoned the energy to lift his head, her satisfied smirk made him incredibly glad he'd made this impromptu visit.

"That was freaking unbelievable." She reached up and touched the dip between his collarbone, trailing a fingertip downward. "Maybe next time you should stay away for two weeks?"

∽

MOUNT CHARLESTON WAS ONLY thirty-five miles northwest of the Vegas Valley, but for Poppy, it might as well have been the moon.

She was sure she was having an out-of-body experience as Beck steered the Maserati up the mountain. While he'd waxed lyrical about the Joshua trees at the lowest level, giving way to cedar and eventually the bristlecone pine in the alpine forest at the top, she'd been completely blissed out, her body still languid from their reunion.

They'd done it three times yesterday morning, twice in the afternoon, and a record four last night. Was it legal to have so many orgasms in one day? Too bad if it was. Arrest her now.

If Beck wasn't so bent on showing her some of the local countryside he seemed to love so much, they could've been holed up in his house right now trying to top yesterday's marathon effort. Then again, she'd spied the king-size picnic blanket in the trunk. All they needed was a secluded spot among all these trees...

"You're awfully quiet." He shot her a quick glance as he pulled over and she stretched, enjoying the way his gaze zeroed in on her T-shirt stretching taut across her chest.

"I was waiting for you to cough up that encyclopaedia you must've swallowed. I couldn't get a word in."

The Beck she'd first met a few weeks ago would've frowned. But the new, improved Beck, the one who seemed to have enjoyed yesterday as much as she had, shook his head with a tolerant grin. "It's good for you to see there's more to Vegas than bright lights and Elvis impersonators."

She rested her hand on his thigh and squeezed. "I know there's more." Her fingers sneaked upward. "A lot more."

"You're a maniac," he said, clamping down on her hand before she hit the jackpot. "But we're not going to make it out of the car if you keep doing that."

"Your point is?" She tried a fake pout for good measure.

"Later." He laughed and unsnapped their seat belts. "I want to show you something."

"Better be special." She earned an amused glance as he vaulted out of the car and grabbed the picnic basket from the backseat.

"Can you get the blanket?"

"Sure thing, scout master." He popped the trunk and she hoisted the heavy blanket onto her shoulder, not fathoming his furtive expression when she slammed the trunk shut.

"It's not far," he said, heading off on a small trail that seemed to rise vertically, leaving her with a tempting view of his butt in faded denim.

"Spoken like a true exercise junkie." She trudged after him in the same way she'd attended every gym class at high school. Reluctantly.

The incline rose rapidly for five minutes before flattening out, leaving them on a secluded plateau with views to die for: rolling hills dotted in greenery, sloping valleys, and a distant lake.

"Wow." She shook out the blanket and spread it, waiting for it to settle before plunking down in exhaustion. "You were right, it was worth it for the view alone."

He didn't answer and when she glanced up, he was looking at her with the strangest expression—half-fear, half-awe.

"If you're thinking of proposing, too late," she said, chuckling at her lame joke.

He didn't laugh. Dumping the picnic basket nearby, he knelt next to her and reached into his pocket. When he pulled out a small purple velvet box from one of Vegas's premier jewelers, her heart backflipped.

"I know you said you didn't want an engagement ring to add to the phoniness, but I think you should have one." He raised the lid and her mouth dropped open as sunlight reflected off the exquisite two-carat princess-cut diamond. "Not many women would have the guts to agree to my crazy scheme, let alone marry me, and you deserve this."

He slid it onto her ring finger where it nestled against the white gold band. "If you don't want to call it an engagement ring, consider it a thank-you gift for being so damned amazing about this whole marriage thing."

She gawked at the stunning diamond, wanting to thank him, wanting to make light of their pretend marriage, but when she finally looked at him, the gratitude clogged in her throat.

For in that moment, this marriage felt far from pretend and all too scarily real.

Tenderness lurked in the shadows of his eyes as he lifted her hand to his mouth and kissed the knuckle above the ring. "You're incredible. I just wanted you to know it."

Now was the time to make a joke about yesterday, and how this was the sex talking. But he couldn't have organized this ring since yesterday, not when they'd been wrapped around each other twenty-four-seven, which meant he'd brought the ring with him.

And it held far more value than she'd given him credit for.

She cleared her throat. "Thank you. I love it."

"Good. Now let's eat." Suddenly brusque, he set out the picnic while she hugged her knees to her chest, unable to tear her gaze away from the ring.

It shouldn't mean so much. That little twist of metal and diamond adorning it signified he felt it, too. A tentative bond fast developing into something deeper—something that terrified her so much she'd rather take a flying leap off this mountainside than acknowledge it.

"Dig in."

She made a grand show of selecting morsels of ricotta and leek tartlet, char-grilled calamari and salmon terrine, shoving them around her plate. But she could barely eat.

He didn't call her on it, considering his plate resembled hers after ten minutes.

"Not hungry?" She pointed to his plate while placing hers on the ground.

"Maybe I lost my appetite. You've worn me out." His bashful grin made her heart twist with the same unusual sensation as when he'd slipped the ring on her finger.

"In that case you better eat to keep up your strength."

She scuttled closer to him until their thighs touched. "You'll need it for later."

She half expected him to kiss her, maybe strip her and use sex as a way to ease the awkwardness that had descended since he gave her the ring. Instead, he slid an arm around her waist and hugged her tight, leaving her no option but to snuggle.

"I discovered this place my first six months in Vegas." He wrapped his other arm around her when she rested her head on his shoulder. "The hacienda wasn't built yet and I needed to escape the city on weekends, so I started exploring. Lake Mead, Hoover Dam, Grand Canyon, here... I scoured every inch."

"Closet environmentalist, huh?"

"I like the open spaces. They soothe me." He paused and she stayed silent, sensing he had more to say. "I lived in a trailer when I was a kid. Then my folks headed to Vegas for a while and we lived in this squalid single-room apartment downtown."

Beck inclined his head at the view stretching for miles in front of them. "When you live in confined quarters, open spaces become important."

His honesty made her eyes burn with the sting of unshed tears. She'd never expected him to open up emotionally and hot on the heels of the ring, it was almost too much. An intimacy she hadn't expected, an intimacy she feared.

"When they OD'd, Pa took me in and while we lived in a trailer, he understood the need for space. He took me hiking and we camped out in the desert, where I'd stare at the stars for hours."

Beck tipped his head back and gazed at the canopy above, and she imagined a young boy doing whatever it took to survive, hanging onto the dreams of one day exploring the open spaces.

"You must think I'm a sad case, using a fake marriage to get ahead in business, but I had enough of people looking down on me growing up, people judging me, forming wrong opinions." He hugged her tighter, like a kid with a security blanket. "I won't tolerate it now, which is why I need to make this deal happen using whatever means at my disposal."

She didn't know whether to be relieved or disappointed he'd refocused on what he did best: business. "It's that important to you?"

"I dragged you into this mess, didn't I?" His bark of laughter was devoid of humor. "That'll tell you how far I'd go."

"Hey, we all have our motivations for doing what we do."

"Your sister?" He eased off on the hug, sliding a hand up her back to stroke her hair.

"Yeah, she's a mess. Her husband"—Poppy made air quotes—"*fell out of love*, apparently, and walked out on her. She had no idea it was coming. The jerk bought a red sports car and cruises around Provost like he has a new lease on life, while Sara..."

"What?"

"She spiraled into a deep depression. Been on heavy meds, and she's in a rehab clinic trying to recover. She's improving, but the business is all she has left, and if anything happened to it—"

"It's why you started the divorce diva, isn't it? Inject new life into her business?"

"Yeah, but that's the irony. Sara would have a fit if she knew I was doing it. She said as much when I went to tell her we were getting married. She despises the idea, probably because she'll be going through it shortly, hence the anonymity."

"Your secret's safe with me." He kissed her on the top of her head and she sighed.

"She practically raised me. My folks were too caught up in their careers and each other to care about us."

"Makes you wonder why parents like ours have kids in the first place, huh?"

"Damned straight."

Silence stretched between them, but this time it was comfortable, not awkward.

In sharing their private thoughts, they'd bonded far beyond any ring. For the first time ever, Poppy had let a guy get close enough to form a real connection. And shockingly, it didn't send her into a tailspin.

As he held her tight, his silent strength so appealing, she had to admit she liked it.

TWELVE

Divorce Diva Daily recommends:
Playlist: "Beat It" by Michael Jackson
Movie: Broadcast News
Cocktail: Pick-Me-Up

Beck put his game face on, the same one he'd used to great effect growing up.

Every time his folks promised him a Christmas gift and forgot. Every time they missed his birthday. Every time he came home to find no food on the table and welfare shot up their arms.

Then there were the countless times at school when he pretended every jibe, every putdown, every taunt didn't hurt. Yeah, he'd become an expert of the game face from an early age and it had served him well in business. He didn't play poker, but if he did, he'd win a squillion.

He squared his shoulders and strode into the boardroom, ready to kick some corporate ass.

This deal was his. He'd used whatever means necessary, including marrying a woman he was fast developing feelings for. A woman with the potential to undermine him far better than any business rival.

As eight assessing stares swung his way, he quit thinking about Poppy. Time enough to contemplate his complicated personal life later.

"Thanks for coming, gentlemen."

A few nodded, while Stan, the unofficial spokesperson, stood and shook his hand. "Looking forward to hearing what you have to say, Blackwood."

Beck nodded and Stan resumed his seat. The irony wasn't lost on Beck. The investors had already heard what he had to say, basically salivated at the deal he'd put forward. If it hadn't been for his site manager's indiscretion and the investors' old-school mentality, he wouldn't have to go through any of this. But he would. He'd jump through their metaphorical hoops and add a cartwheel for good measure to secure this deal.

He jabbed at a few buttons on his laptop and brought up a new presentation, a rehashing of the old with some minor adjustments. For the next thirty minutes he used his game face to great effect, adding animation when needed, producing the right enthusiasm to wow.

Judging by the enthusiastic applause and general back-slapping by the end of his presentation, he'd succeeded. There were no questions. He hadn't expected any. They'd all been asked last time. When the group collectively looked toward Stan for guidance, Beck inadvertently held his breath.

"You made some good points today, Blackwood. Expanded on your proposal from last time." Stan paused and glanced around the group, making a grand show of equanimity. "What do you think, gentlemen? This proposal looks solid to me."

Murmurs of agreement filtered through the room and Beck exhaled in relief.

"I think we've got ourselves a deal."

Beck resisted the urge to punch the air in victory. He settled for a sedate handshake with Stan and the other investors before they scuttled out.

He'd done it. Achieved a lifelong goal. To make people sit up and take notice, to look at him with respect, not derision.

The faster he got Stan's signature on the dotted line, the faster he could get back to Poppy and celebrate.

"You did good, better than the other contender." Stan gathered up his things. "Your company has cleaned up its act and so have you."

Inwardly Beck seethed. One indiscretion by an employee and people like Stan tarnished his company. As for him, he'd never been all that wild to begin with, but amazing what a convenient marriage could do for a guy's reputation.

"Come by my office Monday and I'll sign off on the deal."

Beck's internal happy dance faltered. "I've got the documents ready to go now."

Stan stared at him as if he'd asked him to sign a new Declaration of Independence. "My attorney will need to look it over again, in case you've made amendments."

"I haven't," Beck said, his tone modulated when he felt like yelling in frustration.

"Good. Then it shouldn't take long and we'll be ready to proceed Monday."

Beck had no choice. He'd be happier when the entire

deal was signed, sealed, and delivered, but it was merely a formality. In high-end business, a man's word was as good as a promise, so he'd sit tight over the weekend and wait.

"Shall we say eleven Monday morning?" Beck asked.

"Sure."

Beck escorted Stan to the door, grateful he had Poppy to distract him over the next forty-eight hours. He would've gone stir-crazy otherwise, watching the clock and waiting for Monday to roll around.

Stan paused at the door. "You'll be at the party tomorrow night?"

Stan made it sound like he'd be attending a brothel rather than Lou's divorce party.

"Yeah, so will most of LA and Vegas, from what I hear."

Stan frowned. "Rather crass, don't you think? Celebrating divorce?"

Beck had no intention of getting into a moral argument with the sanctimonious do-gooder, especially when he was this close to securing his deal. "Lou sees it as celebrating his new life, not the divorce."

Stan's bushy brows shot heavenward. "People should work harder at their marriages, not walk at the first sign of trouble."

Great. Beck could only imagine the lectures he'd cop when his divorce came through. The twinge in his chest was surprising. Conscience? Or something deeper? Something involving him and Poppy extending their marriage contract for a little longer... "Guess that's up to the individuals. No one knows what goes on behind closed doors."

"True." Stan pinned him with a probing stare. "How's married life treating you?"

"Couldn't be better."

"Good to hear." Stan leaned closer, like he was about to

impart some long lost secret. "Your newfound stability went a long way to convincing the investors to sign."

"Really?" How Beck managed to say it with a straight face he'd never know.

"Yeah, more people should focus on marriage rather than divorce." Stan shook his head. "Nasty business, but my wife wants to attend the party and what the boss says goes."

Thank goodness Poppy had insisted on preserving her anonymity. Beck had a feeling even his marriage wouldn't have been enough to save this deal if Stan and his conservative cronies discovered his wife was the one "perpetuating the crassness."

"I'll see you tomorrow, then." Beck ushered him out the door, his patience at a limit.

"That you will." Stan slapped him on the back one last time for good measure and Beck hid his distaste.

He'd have to tolerate the buffoon for the duration of this deal, but thankfully once construction started in the various states across the country, Stan would be part of the behind-the-scenes moneymen and Beck wouldn't have to deal with him much.

When Stan disappeared behind the elevator doors, Beck's PA glanced up from her desk with a raised eyebrow. He gave a thumbs-up and she grinned.

He'd done it. Facilitated the deal of a lifetime for his company. And every state across the southern US would soon know who Beck Blackwood was. He should be rounding up his crew and heading to Blackwood's for a round of drinks...or ten.

Instead, he glanced at his watch, wondering how much longer it would take Poppy to arrive. He had the distinct urge to celebrate this deal with the one person who knew how much it meant to him.

His wife. A title he was fast becoming attached to. And rather than the urge to bolt as fast as his jet could fuel up, the idea of being married to her on a more permanent basis was growing on him.

∽

AS POPPY GLANCED around the room, filled with Californian and Nevadan movers and shakers, A-listers, and a few B-grade movie stars beneath a fairy-light star-studded blue velvet sky, she knew she'd done good.

She'd gone all out for this party and it showed, from the ice-carved hearts to the fifteen-piece big band, the silver and navy color scheme, to the Michelin-starred hors d'oeuvres.

People would be talking about Lou Robinson's divorce party for a long time to come.

In turn, Sara's business would boom. Once she let her sis in on the secret, of course.

Plenty of time for that. For now, she'd continue building clientele, Beck would become the biggest name in high-end construction America had ever seen, and they'd continue to grow closer. And that was really what had her floating tonight. Sure, a successful party was important, but not half as important as realizing the guy she'd married had opened her eyes to a world of possibilities.

Namely, it was okay to risk your heart for a guy...if he was the right one. And that was exactly what she was on the verge of doing, if she hadn't already done it.

She'd fallen a little bit in love with her husband last weekend on that mountaintop, a feeling that had only intensified since. Seven days was a long time to miss someone, and the only thing that had stopped her from leaving Red

Rock Canyon and heading to Vegas was her own stupid insecurities.

What if he didn't feel the same way?

What if the ring he'd given her had been exactly as he said, a thank-you gift?

What if she laid it all on the line, only to end up as devastated as her sister?

Then she'd arrived last night and he'd gone a long way to alleviate her doubts.

Rather than celebrating his deal's success with a lavish dinner surrounded by his colleagues as she'd expected, he'd switched off his phone and they'd holed up in his penthouse, feasting on gourmet pizza and each other. And they'd talked some more, sharing their respective childhoods, strengthening the fragile emotional bond they'd established last weekend, until she could've quite happily stayed in his arms forever.

She'd still be there, too, locked in his embrace, if she hadn't had to work like a maniac today to confirm every party detail so she had to do nothing tonight but mingle like a guest. Ashlee was supposed to run interference for the party, being the staff's go-to person, but her BFF had pulled out early this morning citing a migraine. Odd, considering her friend rarely had a headache. But Poppy hadn't had time to ponder Ashlee's excuse, considering she'd run around all day ensuring this party rocked.

Thankfully it did, and as the big band launched into a Sinatra medley, she sighed with contentment. In another few hours she would secure twenty grand for Divorce Diva Daily and have enough new business to keep busy. When not lusting after her husband.

"Great party." Speak of the devil. Beck slid his arms around her waist from behind.

She tilted her face up to receive his kiss. "Thanks. I hear this diva chick is hot property in the party planning biz."

"She's hot property, period," he said, nuzzling her neck until her skin pebbled. He held her tighter, and her butt encountered evidence of how hot he found her.

"Hold that thought," she said, wriggling against him, empowered when he groaned.

"Stop, you're killing me."

"Not yet, but the night is young." She winked and turned in the circle of his arms, draping her arms around his neck. "I'm glad Lou chose a love theme for this party. Shows he's not some bitter cynic."

"Yeah, gotta hand it to him, the big guy's a romantic schmuck."

She laughed at his mock wince. "Makes me think there's hope for the rest of us." Hope for them. And that was what she wanted to tell Beck later. Poppy was done pretending this marriage meant nothing beyond business. Time to make their relationship real.

She waited for him to disengage, to pull away on the pretext of greeting a long-lost buddy. Instead, his hold on her waist tightened as he met her stare dead-on.

"Yeah, who would've thought, a confirmed cynic like me could have his mind changed by an incredible woman?"

Poppy's heart leaped. "Are you saying—"

"There you two are. I've been looking for you everywhere."

Silently cursing Stan Walkerville's rotten timing, she dragged up a smile for the old guy. By the glower on Beck's face as he released her, he was just as annoyed by Stan's interruption. "Enjoying yourself?"

Stan frowned and jabbed a finger in Beck's direction. "I don't take kindly to being made a fool of."

To Beck's credit, he didn't blink. In fact, his expression didn't change at all and she admired his ability to maintain a poker face when she would've been tempted to sock the guy for speaking to them in that patronizing tone. "Not sure what you mean—"

"This party," Stan hissed, spittle forming at the corners of his mouth. "You knew what I thought of this celebrating divorce rubbish yet here you are, smack bang in the thick of it."

Unease crept down Poppy's spine but she dismissed it as being overcautious. She gripped Beck's hand and held on just in case.

"Lou's my CFO and a good friend. I had to be here—"

"You know what I'm talking about." Stan's narrow-eyed glare swung her way. "Turns out your wife is perpetrating this divorce abomination and you're both choosing to hide the fact."

Poppy swayed as her blood pressure dropped, the shock of Stan's revelation ripping through her earlier confidence. That had been her problem, being too happy. With the job she'd done here, with the diva business, with her marriage. Pride falls and all that.

"Let's go discuss this somewhere more private—"

"No." Stan took a step closer and Beck held his ground. "There's nothing to discuss. Either your wife stops this revolting business or our deal is off. Got it?"

Beck showed the first signs of emotion, tension pinching his mouth. "Let's be reasonable—"

"I am." Stan jerked a thumb over his shoulder at his wife, surrounded by a posse of equally nipped and tucked middle-aged women. "Bessie's a senior minister in our church. I can't be seen associating with anything distasteful, which is why I nixed your deal in the first place."

Beck opened his mouth to respond but Stan held up his hand. "You're a smart businessman, Blackwood, but my patience is running thin. This is your last chance."

He jabbed a pudgy finger in Poppy's direction. "Get your wife under control or kiss our deal good-bye."

Stan gave them both one last death glare for good measure before stalking away.

"How the hell did he find out?" Poppy asked.

Beck stared at her, wild-eyed. "Do you think that matters?" He swore and released her hand. "I've worked on this frigging deal for eighteen months and now it's all down the toilet because of…"

He didn't need to complete the sentence. His body language and inability to look at her spoke volumes. Despite the fact that he'd put her in an untenable position, forcing her to accept his proposal, he blamed her business for this. Irrationally blamed her, when he'd been in control of this fiasco right from the very beginning.

And in that moment, with her heart aching and the slow burn of tears stinging her eyes, she knew exactly why she hadn't let any guy get this close before.

Love hurt like a bitch.

Uh-oh. She *loved* him? Sheesh, the good times just kept on rolling.

"Go on, say it. It's because of me."

He shook his head and turned away. She had her answer right there.

"Don't you dare turn your back on me after all I've done for you."

He glanced over his shoulder, incredulity warring with anger. "Yeah, you've been a real girl scout. Altruistic. Not doing any of this for your own benefit."

A torrent of furious, hurtful retorts bubbled up and

threatened to spill from her lips, so she clamped them shut. They'd already garnered a few curious glances from partygoers nearby, and no way would she give them fodder for tomorrow's gossip columns.

"This isn't the place." She snagged his arm and half dragged him away from the revelers. "Let's go sort this out." They headed for the door, and it irked that even at a time like this, he managed to paste a smooth smile on his face for the crowd.

The consummate performer. And that's when it hit her. He'd been playing her all along. The ring, the divulging of past truths, the time spent together—it was all a lie. A ruse by a player who had an objective in mind and would do anything to achieve it. Once the deal had been inked, he still needed her beside him, playing the dutiful wife, demonstrating to his precious investors he was the man for the job.

Well, screw them. And screw him.

"In here." She opened the door to a supply closet and yanked him inside. When he didn't say anything, merely stared at her with blank, cool indifference, she lost it.

"What's it going to be? Your wife or your all-important deal?"

"Calm down." His icy tone raised goose bumps of trepidation and she surreptitiously rubbed her arms. "I can't think with you carrying on like a banshee."

"*Banshee?*" Of course her voice screeched like one and she curled her fingers into her palms to stop from slugging him. "I told you how important it was for me to remain anonymous. Yet here we are, with that pompous jackass knowing everything and threatening you."

She wrapped her arms around her middle and hugged

tight. Yeah, like that would stop the pain. "How the hell did he find out?"

"Who frigging cares? Everything I've worked so hard for is in the balance." He slammed the wall with his fist and she silently applauded. At last, some sign of emotion. "There's only one solution here."

She knew what was coming before he spoke and it saddened her beyond belief that he'd expect it of her. "What's that?"

"Shut down Divorce Diva."

"Go to hell." She thrust her chin up, eyeballed him. "Sara can't lose her business."

"She won't lose. Name your price. I'll pay you whatever it's worth in lost revenue—"

"No."

One syllable, deadly cool, deadly calm, when inside she seethed with so many emotions she could've launched herself at him and shaken him until he understood. Not that it would do any good. If he didn't get it now, he never would.

"No?" His incredulous expression was that of a man not familiar with being refused anything.

"Is that your solution to everything? Throw a few million at the problem, hope it'll go away?" She stepped into his personal space, resisting the urge to throttle him. "Need a wife? Easy, fling half a mill at her. Need her to go away? Fling some more."

She jabbed at his chest, hating how she registered how rock hard it felt at a time like this. "News flash. I can't be bought."

"Really? Because it worked before." She saw he regretted it the moment the accusation spilled from his lips. He swiped a hand across his face as if to erase it. "Sorry, that was a cheap shot—"

"You can stick your apology and your offer up your ass." She made it sound like he'd proposed to give her the plague rather than cash. "I married you to save my sister, and yeah, the money is helping. But I thought..." She swallowed the rest of what she was about to say, hating that emotion could cloud her judgment at a time like this.

"What?"

"Never mind." She shook her head, but it did little to shut up her inner voice, the one wishing he'd give up everything—including his precious deal—to be on her side.

"I need this deal to happen." He grabbed her upper arms. "And I need you to help me do it."

"I can't—"

"Then that's it." He released her and stepped back, the cold finality in his tone making her shiver.

"This marriage is over?"

He couldn't meet her disbelieving stare, his glassy gaze fixed on some point over her right shoulder. "Whatever you think."

All the confusion of the last few weeks—dealing with uncharacteristic emotions including stupid love, marrying in a whirlwind, moving—erupted in a flash of fury. "I think you're scared. So damned terrified of what's been happening between us that you wanted out of this marriage and this is your way of doing it."

"What the—"

"You leaked the Diva info. You knew Stan wouldn't tolerate it. You're running scared."

He finally dragged his gaze to meet hers and the devastation she glimpsed matched hers. "You're not making sense. I need this marriage to work—"

"Wrong. Once you signed that deal you wouldn't need

me at all. But you screwed up. You thought you'd sign the deal today and I'd be out of your hair come Monday. Too bad for you Stan changed the deadline and your leak worked against you."

"You're crazy." He backed away, not having far to go until he hit the closet door. "Are you listening to yourself? You're a bundle of contradiction."

Maybe she was. Maybe she was so overwrought at losing the one guy she'd been foolish enough to fall in love with that her brain had entered meltdown. But she couldn't stand here one second longer and participate in her marriage falling apart. A marriage that suddenly meant more to her than she could've ever thought possible.

She squared her shoulders and tilted her chin to stare him down. "Well, then, this crazy person better get the hell out of your life so you can get on with what you do best. Make money."

She pushed past him. He grabbed at her arm. "Poppy, wait—"

She brushed him off and with one last withering stare she slipped out of the door, firmly slamming it on her past.

And headed for a future that didn't include obnoxious billionaires who didn't trust her at all.

THIRTEEN

Divorce Diva Daily recommends:
Playlist: "Here I Go Again" by Whitesnake
Movie: Eat, Pray, Love
Cocktail: Morning Glory

Every bone in Beck's body ached, the same way it had after a beating he'd taken from a bully in junior high for daring to challenge him in football. Now, like then, he felt like pummeling something. He wanted to go after Poppy. He should. But that physical beating he'd taken as a kid was nothing like the emotional thrashing he'd just received.

She didn't trust him. The only woman he'd ever let get close, the only woman he'd ever considered a real future with, thought he'd betrayed her. It hurt ten times worse than anything he'd coped with in the past.

His folks had been A-grade losers, so every letdown had been expected. He'd grown immune to the hurt after a while, had perfected an indifference not many people could penetrate.

Poppy had managed to do it in less than a month. "Damn it." This time he did punch something, a stack of hotel linens that absorbed his frustration.

He'd botched this entire situation badly, demanding she give up the business she'd fought so hard to save. How would he have felt if she'd demanded he walk away from his deal for her?

Only one solution. If she wouldn't back down, he'd have to.

Because he couldn't live without her. He'd spent the better part of two years putting this nationwide expansion together, devoted countless hours and money to ensuring this deal would be the crowning glory for Blackwood Enterprises. His name in every business journal, newspaper, and magazine across the country for being the desert king with the Midas touch.

Would he give it all up for a woman? Could he? He'd been so close to declaring his jumbled feelings when Stan interrupted, had seen the answering spark of something deeper in her eyes. Could he hang his hopes that she felt the same way he did, and that's why she'd overreacted?

She'd been irrational at the end, flinging crazy accusations that didn't make sense.

Beck needed this marriage to work even after the deal went through, though technically she'd been right. Once Stan signed and the cooling-off period lapsed, there wasn't anything the investors could do without losing a small fortune, something they wouldn't do, since they were businessmen first and foremost.

He'd intended on ending the marriage when the time was right.

The way he felt now, that time would be never. But first, he had to do some serious work to ensure he didn't lose everything, including his business...and his girl.

∽

POPPY COULDN'T GET AWAY from Beck fast enough. Which was how she found herself unlocking the back door of Party Hard's offices at three a.m.

She'd taken the red-eye to LA with nothing but the slinky chartreuse cocktail dress on her back and a clutch containing ninety-seven bucks. Maxing out her credit card to grab a last-minute seat had been worth it to escape Vegas. And him.

Stupid thing was, even as she'd fidgeted at the boarding gate, she'd half expected to see him vaulting the check-in desk to stop her. And half wanted it to happen, too.

Crazy. Because if he'd wanted to, he would've come after her at the party. But he hadn't, effectively ending her happily-ever-after fantasy.

Though she'd done a good job of ending that herself. She'd acted like a lunatic, accusing him of leaking her identity to escape their relationship, when every caress, every gesture lately had indicated he wanted the opposite. Though he had demanded she give up the business. And what had he said before Stan interrupted them? Something about her being incredible and changing his mind.

Yeah, she'd botched this big time. But maybe it was better this way. End it after a month of marriage before she got in any deeper? Though how much deeper could she get than falling in love?

She stubbed her toe on the edge of Sara's desk and bit

back a yell. Silver-spangly peep pumps were no match for wrought iron.

Fumbling her way to the back room, she flipped a switch. And screamed. A figure brandishing a baseball bat leaped at her from behind the door and she kicked out, realizing a second too late the action would only serve to increase the throbbing in her toe.

She howled with pain as the intruder said, "Poppy? Is that you?"

"What the…" Hopping around on one foot, Poppy bumped into Ashlee and sent them both toppling onto the nearby sofa. Sofa bed. Which was currently a bed with a body-shaped indent where her best friend had just been. "Why are you sleeping here?"

Ashlee glanced at the sofa bed and Poppy knew her best friend well enough to imagine her trying to come up with a fast excuse. "Would you believe Craig's place has rodents?"

Poppy shook her head. "Try again."

"How about an infestation of bed bugs?"

"Nope, still not buying it."

Ashlee sighed and sank onto the mattress. "We broke up."

"*What?*" Poppy collapsed beside her. She hadn't thought anything could snap her out of her own misery tonight. She'd thought wrong. "I can't believe this."

"Believe it," Ashlee spat out, her fiery retort belied by the hurt in her eyes. "Apparently my rat bastard ex-fiancé is going through some kind of mid-life crisis twenty years too early."

"I don't understand…"

"Neither do I." Tears filled Ashlee's eyes and spilled down her cheeks. "One minute we're choosing flower arrangements for the church, the next he's telling me he needs space." She held up a shaky hand and ticked off points. "Taking a trip to Hawaii. Changing his job. Buying a new car."

Poppy didn't want to ask, but it was the obvious question. "Another woman?"

Ashlee shrugged. "Who knows? Not like he'd admit it."

"I'll kill him." Poppy draped an arm across Ashlee's shoulders and squeezed. "Say the word and I'll put a hit out."

Ashlee's wobbly smile cut through her tears. "Thanks, but then he won't get to see me moving on with some hot stud with a bigger..." She wiggled her pinkie and Poppy hugged her harder.

"Could've been worse," Poppy said.

"You think?"

"You could've found out after the wedding."

"Yeah, but then I would've had a bunch of sensational toasters and tea kettles to comfort me."

"You're cracking jokes. That's a good sign."

Ashlee plucked at the hem of her T-shirt. "Want to know the worst part?"

"Does it involve Craig wearing women's underwear?"

Ashlee snorted. "I never want to picture that jerk naked again, let alone in satin panties."

Poppy winced. "Sorry. Just trying to lighten the mood. What were you going to say?"

"The worst part of our breakup?" Ashlee's gaze shifted. "I'm more upset about moving out of his cool apartment than losing him."

Wow. Poppy had always thought Ashlee and Craig were great together. He could be a little anal at times, but he balanced her bubbly friend nicely. They complemented each other and she hadn't been surprised when they'd moved in together after six months and got engaged twelve weeks after that.

To learn that a relationship she assumed rock-solid wasn't only reinforced what she already knew: love sucked.

"Can't believe I've become one of those cliché fiancées, more in love with love itself than the guy I was about to pledge my life to." Ashlee's bitter laugh ended on a sob. "What a sap."

"Hey, you two were great while it lasted. Focus on the good stuff."

"I guess." Ashlee sniffled and Poppy plucked a tissue from a box on the table and handed it to her. "You don't mind me crashing here, 'til I find a new place?"

"'Course not. Though you could've told me."

"And interrupt your Vegas honeymoon?"

Vegas. Honeymoon. What a joke. "I'm your BFF. You should've..."

Realization struck. When Ashlee had pulled out of Lou's divorce party, deep down Poppy had sensed something was off beyond the migraine excuse. But she hadn't pushed, too wrapped up in her own euphoria.

Selfish. Just like her parents. The two people she'd sworn to never be like.

Maybe that's what love did to people. Made them so egocentric and focused on the object of desire, never mind anybody else.

"What's wrong?" As if noticing her for the first time, Ashlee pointed at her dress. "And why are you wearing that?"

Poppy knew once Ashlee got on a roll she wouldn't stop. "Hang on, why are you even here? It's three in the morning."

When Poppy clamped her lips shut and didn't respond,

Ashlee threw her hands up in disgust. "Not you, too. Let me guess, you and The Hottie broke up."

"Inevitable, don't you think, considering our marriage wasn't real in the first place?"

"You're kidding, right?" Ashlee's raised eyebrows almost hit her hairline. "All that 'just business' and 'convenience' crap might've been your motivation at the start, but I saw how you two looked at each other. You were crazy in love."

"Lust, not love, and sometimes it's not enough."

Ashlee's hand flew to her mouth. "Uh-oh, you said the L-word and you never say the L-word."

"Figure of speech." Damn, her voice gave a betraying wobble and predictably Ashlee latched onto it.

"Bull. Want to know what I think?"

"Not really—"

"You've fallen for him. You wouldn't be here in the middle of the night otherwise..." Ashlee snapped her fingers. "Hang on a sec. Lou's divorce party was tonight. No way in Hades you would've abandoned that without good reason, which proves I'm right."

Smugly, she folded her arms and nodded. "You wouldn't have bolted unless something major went down and to care that much, you must love him."

"Finished, Dr. Phil?"

"Hey, focusing on you made me forget about Craig for a few minutes." Ashlee's mouth twisted into a wry grin. "Psychoanalyzing you is like free therapy for me."

"Sorry to burst your Freudian bubble, but nothing major went down." Poppy mentally apologized for the white lie. "We realized we want different things, so what's the point in perpetuating the sham?"

Ashlee peered at her, a frown slashing her brows. "The point is, you're full of it."

"Leave it—"

"No." Ashlee leaped up and propped herself on the table opposite, leaving Poppy no option but to meet her scrutinizing gaze head on. "Tell me you don't love him."

I don't love him hovered on Poppy's lips, but she couldn't do it, couldn't lie to her best friend. Next to Sara, Ashlee was the only other person she truly trusted, and no way would she let some guy make her lie. "So what if I do?"

Ashlee squealed and jumped up and down. "I knew it. About freaking time."

"Uh, don't you find this a little odd, that I fall for a guy I married for his money?"

Ashlee waved away her concern. "Not really. The Real Housewives of someplace county do it all the time."

Poppy smiled, even though it was the last thing she felt like doing. "This isn't a reality show."

"Then cut the drama." Ashlee knelt in front of her and clasped her hands. "Whatever happened between you two, sort it out."

Poppy sent a pointed glance at Ashlee's bare ring finger with the faint tan line. "This from the woman who walked away from an engagement?"

As Ashlee's eyes filled with tears again, Poppy silently cursed her insensitivity. "Sorry, Ash—"

"There's a massive difference between walking away from a guy who doesn't want you and one who does."

"Beck doesn't want me—"

"What if he came marching through that door right now? Would that prove he wants you? Is that what you need, some grand gesture because you're too damn scared to admit the truth?"

Poppy shook her head. It didn't clear the fog. "I'm not hanging myself out here. He specified no emotions from the start. And he certainly hasn't given any declarations of undying affection."

But he had. In his own way. She'd marveled how a guy who'd been born to druggie parents and had it rough as a kid could be so giving and open with her. He may not have said it in words, but his actions had spoken clearly.

In comparison, she hadn't told him much at all. She'd vaguely alluded to her parents' narcissism and she'd given him snippets about Sara only because it tied into her motivation for marriage.

What had she really shared with him, apart from her body?

He'd made the effort to spend time with her, making regular trips to Red Rock Canyon. He'd opened up to her about his past in a way she hadn't expected. He'd been proud of her at the party earlier while respecting her wish for anonymity.

And what had she done? Accused him of being an underhanded sneak, leaking her diva identity to end their marriage as an easy "get out of jail free" card?

"What are you thinking?"

Poppy rubbed her forehead where the beginnings of a headache pounded to life. "I'm thinking your philosophizing is starting to get to me."

"You've got a special guy, hon. I'd hate to see you lose him over pride or stubbornness." Ashlee stood and patted her shoulder. "Now if you don't mind, I need to get back to bed. You took ten years off my life coming in here."

"What's with the baseball bat?"

The cheeky grin Poppy had loved since high school creased Ashlee's face. "It was Craig's prized possession, next to his metrosexual moisturizer."

Poppy laughed. "And he let you have it?"

"What he doesn't know won't hurt him." Ashlee picked up the bat and assumed a hitter's position. "When he's freaked out enough I might ransom it for his new Mustang."

"Good luck with that."

Ashlee placed the bat down and plopped onto the bed. "What would you trade to have Beck back?"

Good question. Poppy had a feeling she'd be pondering it for a long time to come.

Like forever.

∽

"YOUR WIFE CAME through for me in a big way." Lou brandished four business cards under Beck's nose. "Not only does the crème de la crème of LA and Vegas society think I'm a classy guy for throwing such a loved-up divorce party, I managed to get the phone numbers of four hot babes desperate to comfort me."

Beck barely glanced up from his laptop where he went over figures for the final time before they touched down in LA. "Four? Seriously? You could barely handle one woman, and look how that turned out."

"After what you've just 'fessed up, I could say the same about you, big guy." Lou slid the cards in his top pocket and patted it. "At least I wasn't lame enough to chase my woman all the way to LA—"

Beck fixed Lou with a death glare that just made him laugh.

"You think your plan's foolproof?"

Jeez, Beck sure hoped so. "I've anticipated every scenario, so I'm hoping for a positive outcome."

Lou's laughter gave way to guffaws. "You sound like

you're pitching for a construction deal, not trying to save your marriage."

Beck had to compartmentalize this, otherwise he'd go frigging insane.

It had killed him waiting until morning to follow Poppy, but at least he'd used the time wisely, putting into place contingency plans he hoped would convince her of the truth.

He couldn't live without her.

"There you go again with the goofball look." Lou pulled a cross-eyed face. "Never would've believed it if I hadn't seen it with my own eyes. Eligible bachelor extraordinaire takes a dive over the divorce diva. That'd make nice headlines."

Something shifted in the back of Beck's mind. Aligned. Clicked into place. "You met with Stan to go over the figures again after I left him on Friday."

"Yeah."

"Did you mention Poppy at all?"

"Not really." Lou narrowed his eyes, trying to think. "Once we'd been over the figures, Stan was suitably impressed. I was pretty pumped and he started making small talk, so we chatted for a while about general stuff."

"Like?"

"Basketball. Golf. My divorce party."

Beck had a bad feeling, the same kind of feeling that tripped down his spine the day his folks had been discovered dead. "What about the divorce party?"

"The uptight prick was raving on about morals and the sanctity of marriage and the like, so I told him he didn't need to worry, the party was in good hands and it'd be elegance all the way."

"Did you mention Poppy?"

"Of course not." Lou's quick look away told him otherwise.

"What did you say?"

Lou winced. "I may have let slip that Poppy's sister was in the party planning business—"

"You putz. Stan's a sharp guy. That's all he would've needed to do a little research to discover the truth. My PI found the link easily enough, Stan would've too. What were you thinking?"

"I wasn't?" Lou offered, a study in bashful apology. "Look, man, I'm sorry, it just slipped out and I didn't think—"

"No, you didn't." Beck closed his laptop and slid it into its case. "I hope you won't make the same mistake when we land."

"I've got this covered." Lou darted a nervous glance at his briefcase. "Trust me."

"Famous last words," Beck muttered, ignoring the nervous churning in his gut.

This plan had to work. The pitch of his life. One deal he wouldn't consider losing.

"Make sure you stick to the plan, okay? No improvising. No fuck-ups. Got it?"

"It'll be a cinch."

Beck wished he had half Lou's confidence.

FOURTEEN

Divorce Diva Daily recommends:
Playlist: "Someone Like You" by Adele
Movie: Bridesmaids
Cocktail: Pussy Cat

Poppy knew she had to come clean. She'd botched her own life enough; no way would she add to Sara's woes. Her sister needed to hear the truth about Divorce Diva Daily from her. As for the money, she hoped that prenup was watertight and Sara got the cash she was owed.

Taking a deep breath, she shook out her arms like a prizefighter about to enter the ring and stuck her head around Sara's door. "It's only me."

Sara glanced up from her smartphone and smiled, a genuinely wide grin for the first time in months. "Hey, you, come on in." She spontaneously hugged Poppy, rather than being a limpid recipient, and Poppy's surprise increased.

"You look great."

"I feel great." Sara threw her arms wide and spun around, leaving Poppy gobsmacked.

She hadn't seen her sister this happy in a year. Great news, considering it should ease the blow when she divulged the truth.

As Sara gestured her toward the sofa to take a seat, Poppy got a good look at her sister. Freshly washed and blow-dried shiny hair, hint of mascara and lip-gloss, skinny jeans, and her favorite peacock sweater. She looked incredibly healthy and it gave Poppy hope. Maybe Sara had finally shrugged off the past.

Now if only Poppy could do the same. "I have to tell you something and you're not going to like it."

Rather than Sara's smile disappearing, it widened. "Really? Because nothing can spoil my good mood today."

"This will." Scrounging up her courage, Poppy decided blurting it out would work better than dodging the truth in an attempt to soften the blow. "That Divorce Diva Daily website you mentioned when I visited last month? The one you dissed? I'm running it. Thought it'd be a great idea to complement Party Hard, seeing as divorce parties are so hot right now, but then you said you hated it so I've been keeping it anonymous, and it's earned heaps, but it's time you knew—"

"Hey, slow down. Take a breath." Rather than shouting as Poppy had anticipated, Sara was taking the news surprisingly well. "Maybe I was too hasty. I've been in a pretty bad place, so anything involving the D-word would've probably set me off."

Wow, Poppy mouthed, and Sara laughed. "You've been amazingly supportive, but I think I'm ready to come back to work."

"Really? That's fantastic."

"And you know what? The first party I'm going to plan will be my divorce."

Poppy squealed and reached across to hug Sara. "I'm so proud of you."

"Feeling's entirely mutual." Poppy didn't understand the cryptic twinkle in her sister's astute gaze but hey, she wouldn't question it, not when this had gone way better than anticipated.

"How's your hubby?"

"Good." The lie instantly tumbled from her lips. Enough blunt truths for one day.

"When do I get to meet him?"

Hell. "As soon as you're out of here." Poppy stood, eager to escape before lightning struck her dead on the spot. "Gotta dash. Loads to do."

"Thanks for stopping by." Sara hugged her again but this time she held on longer than normal. "I'm so happy for you."

Great, not telling the truth about the disastrous ending to her marriage with Beck had given her sister another false impression she'd have to tear down at a later date.

Forcing a bright smile, Poppy waved and made a swift exit, completely baffled by her sister's knowing chuckles following her out the door.

BECK PACED the outer office of Party Hard, swiping at stray streamers and glaring at rogue balloons.

With its bright and bouncy theme, from purple 21st birthday balloons to "happy retirement" banners edged in gold, the place's perkiness was enough to give a guy a headache.

He didn't go for frills. He liked no-nonsense, upfront, in-your-face honesty.

Which was why he hoped Poppy welcomed him when she found him here. Because he had a dose of honesty she had to hear.

Beck wrinkled his nose at an offending Halloween witch mask dangling in front of his face, swiping it out of the way when the door opened with an annoying bell tinkle.

The hairs on the nape of his neck snapped to attention as the soft summer breeze brought her light, floral scent in before she entered. He turned slowly, his gut a bunch of nerves. She breezed in, a vision in a red and white gingham summer dress, held up by the flimsiest spaghetti straps begging to be tugged down.

His gaze automatically dipped to her shoes out of habit and he wasn't disappointed. Crimson. Shiny. Towering.

A smile played about his lips as he stepped forward into her line of vision.

She stopped. Paled. Bit her lower lip.

"Hey."

The vulnerability of a moment ago disappeared as she marched toward him, her expression hardening with every step. "You're wasting your time. And mine." She pointed to a stack of paperwork on a minimalist desk. "I've got work to do."

"This won't take long." He broached the distance between them in three short strides, hauled her into his arms, and kissed her.

Correction: ravaged her. He plundered her mouth, desperate to taste her. It wasn't enough. He wanted all of her, naked, warm, and willing, but for now this would suffice.

Her momentary resistance shattered on a groan as she

wrapped her arms around his neck and pressed herself to him. Soft, warm curves beneath his hands. Firm, demanding lips beneath his. She was fire and sass and he couldn't get enough.

His Poppy. He backed her up a little and when her butt hit the desk her leg snaked around his waist, bringing him in tantalizing contact to where he craved to be. Blood thundered in his ears, drowning out all rational thought. He had to have her. Now.

Then she shifted a fraction, breaking off the kiss to gulp in air, and a few seconds was all it took for reality to set in.

This wouldn't win him back his wife. He eased away and dragged a hand through his hair, perturbed by the power she had over him. She took turned on to a whole new level.

"We need to talk."

"That old line?" Her mouth made a cute scoff. "Surely you can come up with better material than that to end our marriage."

"I don't want to end it."

That shocked her into momentary silence, before her mask of deliberate distance slid into place. "Too bad, because I do."

"Bull." She crowded him and he took a step back, needing distance to marshal his thoughts.

"Take away the stupid deal we made and we're good together. You know it. I know it."

A spark of acknowledgment lit her eyes before she deliberately blinked. "That's just sex. Don't let it cloud your judgment."

"Stop doing that. Belittling what we have."

"Had," she corrected, her stare defiant. "This was wrong from the beginning." She waved her hand between them. "You and me? A high-stakes gamble that failed, so let's cut our losses and run."

"You think you can get rid of me that easily?"

"Yeah, it's what you do best, isn't it? Run from your past?"

A cheap shot and one she regretted by her blush. Not that he could blame her for saying it. He had run. Not anymore.

"I'm here, aren't I?" He held his hands out to her, palms up, no tricks up his sleeves. "Not running away, not hiding behind excuses. I'm here because I love you and want to make things right between us."

Her eyes widened at the L-word and her lower lip wobbled a tad before she clamped it tight and shook her head. "Just go."

Seriously rattled by her resolute stubbornness to not entertain the thought of reconciliation, he slid his hand into his jacket pocket and pulled out the folded document he hoped would convince her how he felt.

She glanced at it, curiosity raising one eyebrow, before she eyeballed him. "What do you want me to say? That I acted like a crazy person that night at the party? Fine. I did. And I'm sorry. But you showing up here and saying you love me doesn't change facts."

"Why not?"

"Because...because..." She ended on a half-sob, half-hiccup, before swallowing. "Because I don't trust you."

"Don't or can't?" It killed him, having her doubt him. He tipped up her chin with a fingertip so she had to look at him. "There's a big difference."

She swatted him away. "Stop confusing me."

"Confusion is good." He felt the first stirrings of hope. If she was unraveling before his eyes, it meant she did care a hell of a lot more than she was letting on. "Confusion means you're as perplexed as I am over the speed and intensity with which we fell in love."

"Stop saying that."

Unable to resist, he ducked down and murmured in her ear, "Love, love, love. I. Love. You."

"Damn you." She pummeled his chest and tried to shove him away, but he captured her hands and tugged her close, enveloping her into his arms in a crushing hug that left them both breathless.

He let her cry, battling the monstrous lump of emotion wedged in his throat. He smoothed her back, her hair, whispered soft endearments until her sobs petered out. Only then did he ease back, his heart stalling at the utter bleakness in her eyes.

"I'm not a good relationship person," she murmured, clutching at his jacket lapels like she'd never let go.

He wished.

"I could handle us when we had an end date in mind and it was all about the sex, but then we had to go and complicate it with stupid emotions and it all got too hard and I said those horrible things to you and—"

"Ssh..." He placed a finger against her lips. "Do you love me?"

He held his breath, waiting for a response. What seemed like an eternity later, she nodded and all the air whooshed out of his lungs. "Then we can work out the rest."

She squeezed her eyes shut, as if in pain. "What if love's not enough?"

"It'll have to be."

Her eyelids snapped open to pin him with a doubting glare. "Every relationship I've ever known has been dysfunctional. My folks loved each other, too damn much, and at the expense of their kids. My sis loved her hubby and that didn't stop their relationship from imploding. Hell, even Ashlee just broke up with her fiancé. I don't trust love."

He cupped her face with his hands. "Do you trust me?"

"I don't know."

He didn't release her, leaving her nowhere to look but at him. "I didn't leak your identity to Stan. Lou did that accidentally. I'd never betray you like that."

"I'm sorry." Tears filled her eyes again.

"Hey, I'm scared, too. Love sucked until I met you." His gaze landed on the piece of paper that had fallen from his fingers and tumbled onto her desk. "But you changed everything for me. How I view myself. How I handle emotions. And if you don't believe me, maybe this'll convince you."

He handed her the document, waited impatiently as she unfolded it and read.

Her mouth opened and closed before she finally stared at him in wide-eyed shock. "Is this—it can't be—"

"It is. Equal partnership in Divorce Diva Daily. Whatever financial backing Sara needs, she has it. Lou already approached your sister and she's all for it."

That sneak Sara. So that explained her smirk when she'd told her the truth.

"But what about your deal—"

"I told Stan the deal's off." This time her mouth dropped open and stayed that way. "I've spent my life busting my balls trying to prove to everyone what a big guy I was. Rich. Powerful. Holding all the cards. I wanted to lord it over those people from my past who thought I was worth less than the dirt on my shoes. But you know something?" He tapped his chest. "What you made me feel in here? That's all the recognition I need."

To his shock his eyes misted over and he blinked. "You made me *feel*, Poppy. You. With your exuberance and smiles and love. And I want to spend the rest of my life making sure you know how much I love you back."

This time when she burst into tears, he didn't hug her. He kissed her until she smiled against his mouth. Good. Because he intended on making her smile for the rest of her life.

Want to read about another reluctant bride?
NOT THE ROMANTIC KIND out now!

I'M A MARINE SCIENTIST. *He's a CEO property developer out to ruin my family's coastal legacy.*

He's about to discover how far I'll go to protect what's mine.

Gemma loves her job, protecting the oceans from corporate sharks like Rory. So when the uptight property developer sets his sights on her family's beachside land, what's a woman to do but chain herself to his desk?

Rory hasn't got time for disruptions. He has a lot to prove and that means making Devlin Corp number one in the country. But maybe hiring the beautiful crusader Gemma can help his business? After all, what better way to prove his company is environmentally conscious than having her on staff?

Neither count on their unexpected attraction being stronger than the tides...

Read Nicola's newest feel-good romance DID NOT FINISH.
He's a bestselling author. She's a career-wrecking book reviewer.
Who will lose the plot first?

If you enjoyed **NOT THE MARRYING KIND**,
you'll love
SAPPHIRES ARE A GUY'S BEST FRIEND

and
the **HOT ISLAND NIGHTS** duo

WICKED NIGHTS
WANTON NIGHTS

FREE BOOK AND MORE

SIGN UP TO NICOLA'S NEWSLETTER for a free book!

Read Nicola's feel-good romance **DID NOT FINISH**

Or her gothic suspense novels **THE RETREAT** and **THE HAVEN**

(The gothic prequel **THE RESIDENCE** is free!)

Try the **CARTWRIGHT BROTHERS** duo

FASCINATION

PERFECTION

The **WORKPLACE LIAISONS** duo

THE BOSS

THE CEO

Try the **BASHFUL BRIDES** series

NOT THE MARRYING KIND

NOT THE ROMANTIC KIND

NOT THE DARING KIND

NOT THE DATING KIND

The **CREATIVE IN LOVE** series

THE GRUMPY GUY

THE SHY GUY

THE GOOD GUY

Try the **BOMBSHELLS** series

BEFORE (FREE!)

BRASH

BLUSH

BOLD

BAD

BOMBSHELLS BOXED SET

The **WORLD APART** series

WALKING THE LINE (FREE!)

CROSSING THE LINE

TOWING THE LINE

BLURRING THE LINE

WORLD APART BOXED SET

The **HOT ISLAND NIGHTS** duo

WICKED NIGHTS

WANTON NIGHTS

The **BOLLYWOOD BILLIONAIRES** series

FAKING IT

MAKING IT

The **LOOKING FOR LOVE** series

LUCKY LOVE

CRAZY LOVE

SAPPHIRES ARE A GUY'S BEST FRIEND

THE SECOND CHANCE GUY

Check out Nicola's website for a full list of her books.

And read her other romances as Nikki North.

'MILLIONAIRE IN THE CITY' series.

LUCKY

COCKY

CRAZY

FANCY

FLIRTY

FOLLY

MADLY

Check out the **ESCAPE WITH ME** series.

DATE ME

LOVE ME

DARE ME

TRUST ME

FORGIVE ME

Try the **LAW BREAKER** series

THE DEAL MAKER

THE CONTRACT BREAKER

EXCERPT WICKED HEAT

To save her company, Allegra Wilks must land an island resort's lucrative advertising account. But when a lingerie mishap in the airport leads her into the arms of a wickedly distracting stranger, Allegra's tempted to skip the trip altogether.

The sexy Australian Jett Halcott is fighting for the same account and has just as much to lose, and when a week on the island blurs the line between business and pleasure, it's clear more than their companies are at stake.

CHAPTER ONE

Jett Halcott knew lingerie.

Which meant the tall blonde striding through LAX like she had a bug up her ass, leaving a trail of skimpy, provocative satin and lace spilling from her suitcase, was either a hooker or a Victoria's Secret model.

Either would be fine with him.

He could call out to her and put an end to the sniggers from passengers streaming through the chaotic airport.

But where was the fun in that?

Instead, he scooped up every frivolous scrap that tumbled out of her wheeled luggage, like crumbs for a deviant Hansel ready to gobble the gingerbread all in one go.

He wished.

From what he could see, the blonde looked tempting from behind. Long legs. Sexy ass. Shiny, straight hair halfway down her back that swung with every step she took. Fast strides that lengthened the gap between them.

The lingerie shedder was a go-getter or she was about to miss her plane.

He snagged crotchless ivory lace panties, a black bustier, a red corset, and a tempting assortment of satin thongs and sheer bras from the trail she left behind her, mentally dressing her in each and every one.

Hot damn.

He picked up the pace, dodging weary travelers pushing trolleys laden with luggage, eventually catching up with her after they cleared security.

"Excuse me…" He'd planned on making some smart-ass remark when she turned. Instead, he found himself surprisingly speechless as her eyes connected with his.

Pale, light blue, the color of a glacier he'd seen in New Zealand on a school trip once. Pity her haughty expression matched the unusually striking color.

"Is there a problem?" She glanced at his arms, laden with sexy underthings, and her eyes widened.

"Whatever you're selling, I'm not interested."

"Pity. I think you'd look great in this." He snagged a sheer crimson lace thong and held it out on the tip of his forefinger. "Red's definitely your color."

To his surprise she blushed, before directing a death glare at him, the kind of stare that could freeze a guy into hypothermia.

"Do I need to call security?"

"I don't know. Do you?" He returned the thong to the pile in his arms. "Though I'd prefer a one-on-one fashion parade rather than having an audience."

Her lips thinned into an unimpressed line. "I've got a plane to catch."

"Me, too. Which is why I'm done with my good deed for the day and am returning your belongings."

Before she could reply he thrust the lingerie at her and she reacted quickly, managing to catch the lot before they tumbled to the floor.

"These aren't mine—"

"That's what they all say." He pointed at the small suitcase propped at her feet. "Your zipper's busted.

You've been leaving lingerie all through LAX."

She glanced down at her suitcase and groaned. "I'll kill Zoe."

Just his frigging luck, she had a girlfriend.

She studied the mass of purple, pink, ruby, and black underwear in her arms and wrinkled her nose.

"My friend's idea of a joke, packing this stuff for my honeymoon."

Worse luck, she was married.

Her gaze swung back to him. "Do you think you could give me a hand?"

He waited until a booming boarding call over the loudspeaker finished before responding. "Helping you try them on? Absolutely." He grinned, and for a moment the corners of her mouth curved upward in response.

"I meant could you take a look at that zipper and see if it's fixable." She juggled the lingerie in her arms. "Kinda got my hands full."

"It'll cost you," he said, squatting to take a look at her case. Designer. With a very handy name tag hanging off the handle.

Pity Allegra Wilks was married. She was just how he liked his women. Tall. Cool. Blond. With a kick-ass Californian accent he found incredibly sexy.

"Cost me what?"

He fiddled with the zipper, unsnagged the silk lining caught in its steel teeth, and stood. "A celebratory drink before we catch our respective planes."

"What are we celebrating?"

He smirked. "Your wedding."

And the fact that he'd managed not to kill Reeve, his business partner and former best friend, for costing him the one thing that mattered most.

Maybe he'd reserve that pleasure for the prick if he ever surfaced from his hidey-hole in the Caribbean.

For now, he had the distinct urge to see how far he could push the delightfully aloof Allegra.

"Wedding?" she parroted, staring at him like he'd lost his mind. "I'm not married."

She looked away as she said it, and he wasn't sure if he'd glimpsed regret, sadness, or embarrassment before she did.

Maybe this was his lucky day after all.

"You said your friend packed for your honeymoon?" He gestured to her overflowing arms, his mood taking a turn for the better.

"Not that it's any of your business, but I didn't have time to repack." She squared her shoulders and looked down her snooty nose. "I'm heading to Palm Bay without the groom. No wedding. No honeymoon.

No frigging happy ever after." She gave him a thumbs-up. "South Pacific, here I come, woo-hoo."

He bit back a smile at her sarcasm.

Palm Bay? No way.

He should feel sorry for her. Or the poor schmuck she'd probably ditched before being shackled to a proverbial ball and chain. Instead, his blood fizzed as he tried to contain his elation.

He'd have a good eight hours on the flight to charm her into modeling some of that lingerie when they arrived.

A guy could live in hope.

"You left him at the altar?"

"He left me," she said, sounding surprisingly calm for a woman who'd been ditched.

"Dumb bastard," he said, earning another lip quirk for his bluntness.

"Thanks. I think." She tossed the lingerie into the open suitcase at her feet, zipped it, and straightened to her impressive five nine. "And for fixing that."

"Aren't you going to thank me for saving your lingerie?"

She shrugged. "Considering I won't be wearing any of it, I don't care one way or the other."

He tsk-tsked. "Shame."

She didn't want to ask. He could see the silent battle she waged, curiosity with the urge to tell him to piss off.

Thankfully, her curiosity won out. "Shame about what?"

"A gorgeous woman like you should wear sexy stuff all the time." His gaze started at her feet and swept slowly upward, noting her pearly pink nail polish, white capris, turquoise peasant top, and matching pendant hanging from a white-gold choker.

He didn't linger on the parts he wanted to, like the curve of her hip, her trim waist, her C-cup cleavage.

Plenty of time for that. When she was wearing nothing but the sexy stuff.

Yeah, he was that confident. He had to be; otherwise he'd go frigging insane, thinking about what he'd lost and what he faced when he returned home.

"And a bullshit artist like you should quit while he's ahead," she said, her expression telling him she'd liked his compliment regardless.

A feisty one. Would be just the distraction he needed. "How about that drink?"

Her eyes narrowed to slits of ice. "I didn't agree to it."

"Hmm." He tapped his temple, pretending to think. "Yet I fixed your zipper regardless."

"Thanks," she said, grabbing the suitcase handle so hard he wouldn't be surprised if the thing busted again.

But he spied a fleeting glimmer in her eyes, a glimpse of regret, almost sadness. And he could identify with that.

The mess he'd left in Sydney haunted him, probably as much as her being dumped before her wedding. Which meant they shared an unexpected connection. Wouldn't hurt to commiserate together. He could do with a little up-close-and-personal consoling from someone like her.

He touched her arm. "Where I come from, it's not polite to blow someone off after they've done you a favor."

It had been a flyaway comment but something unimaginable sparked in her eyes, something akin to excitement when he'd said the word blow.

So the bust-up babe wasn't as cool as she liked to

pretend. He could work with that. His cock twitched in agreement.

She rolled her eyes. "Let me guess. You use that Aussie accent to woo women along with spin bull."

"You don't like my accent?"

A faint pink stained her cheeks as she glanced away. "I never said that."

"Is it working?" He took a step closer, invading her personal space. "Are you wooed yet?"

She snorted, but her mouth softened into a semi smile. "It'd take a lot more than a great accent and blatant charm to woo me into doing anything with you."

"Anything?" He lowered his voice, *sotto voce*. "And here I was just hoping for a drink."

He deliberately brushed his arm against hers, enjoying her slight flinch. Which meant she felt the spark underlying their exchange as much as he did. "But I'm definitely up for anything."

He expected her to bristle. To shut off. To shoot him down with a cutting quip and an aloof glare.

What he didn't expect was the flare of heat in her steady gaze as she eyeballed him, and the tip of her tongue to dart out and moisten her bottom lip, an innocuous action that shot straight to his hard-on.

"I really do have a plane to catch—"

"You wouldn't want to leave a guy alone when he's down on his luck, would you?" He sniffed and faked knuckling his eyes. "I could do with a shoulder to cry on and maybe you could, too?"

He threw it out there, taking a chance by appealing to her bruised side. She had to be a tad fragile after being dumped by a dickhead. And considering his flirting was getting him nowhere, it wouldn't hurt to change tack.

Besides, he could do with a little lighthearted repartee and sexy distraction before landing in Palm

Bay. The place where his future would be decided.

"What do you say?" He flashed his best smile as a sweetener, encouraged when he glimpsed the corners of her mouth turning up slightly in response.

"Let's start with that drink and see what else you can charm me into," she said, giving the suitcase handle an impatient jiggle as if she couldn't wait.

"Lady, you've got yourself a deal."

They were in for a long flight to Palm Bay and he had more than charming her on his mind.

∽

While her lingerie savior followed up on a problem with his boarding pass, Allegra entered the bar. She'd kill Zoe for packing that lingerie. She knew it was her best friend's idea of a joke, wanting to spice up Allegra's honeymoon on Palm Bay. Ironic, in twenty-four hours her wedding had been canceled, the honeymoon ditched, but a more compelling reason for heading to Palm Bay had presented itself.

A reason that could make or break her business.

She'd had no intention of heading to Palm Bay, despite Flint's insistence that she should enjoy the trip. Her ex-fiancé had good intentions, but the last thing she felt like doing after her aborted wedding was take a week in the sun. Until an hour after they'd broken up, when a giant mother-effing cloud dumped on her and AW Advertising had lost its biggest account.

She'd done everything for one of the largest farms in California, from a national OJ campaign to a statewide billboard spread for its avocados along every highway. Her entire company operated on the profits from the farm mob. And now it was gone. In less than thirty seconds she'd gone from having a successful yet modest advertising agency to being on the skids.

Which meant she needed to secure a new mega-client. A client like Kaluna Resorts, currently seeking a new ad campaign, and her sole reason for heading to Palm Bay. Kai Kaluna was legendary in the hotelier business. He bought small, secluded islands and turned them into six-star luxury resorts for those lucky enough to afford it. Lush hotels and villas frequented by rock stars, movie stars, and supermodels who wanted to be pampered in complete privacy. She'd seen full-page ads for his resorts in glossy travel magazines, had admired his concepts, and envied the ad agency responsible for boosting his profile.

AW Advertising had to be that agency. He'd won awards across the globe for his stunning, eco-friendly resorts, and running an advertising campaign for him would be worth millions. Millions she now needed for her business to survive. If she landed Kaluna, along with several new clients she'd pitched for two weeks ago, her agency would be okay. The smaller clients would provide a much-needed cash injection but it was Kaluna she had to land.

Allegra perched on a barstool, ordered a gin and tonic for her, a beer for the hottie, and wondered what the hell she was doing. Bad enough her reluctant groom had ditched her and business had taken a massive turn for the worse. But now she'd agreed to have a drink with a stranger, something she never did.

Allegra didn't trust many people. She especially didn't trust a slick charmer with bad boy tattooed all over his broad chest. He even wore the requisite bad boy outfit: thigh-hugging black denim, chest-skimming ebony T-shirt, and cowboy boots. Though in all fairness it wasn't his fault she had a thing for Alex O'Loughlin and the hottie happened to bear a striking resemblance to the u¨ber-sexy Australian actor.

That mussed brown hair, unusual green eyes, and day-old stubble did it for her in a big way. Along with the lean, hard bod, the ripped abs, the firm ass…she squirmed. Throw in the easy-on-the-ears Aussie drawl, and how could she say no?

Besides, this was only one drink before she boarded a plane for a week of stress-filled strategizing to nail the pitch of her life.

Plan A, where she married Hollywood producer Flint Dunbar, gained notoriety for her advertising agency, and marketed some of the biggest films in Tinseltown? Gone.

While she lamented the loss of a professional boost, she was secretly relieved that Flint had called off their wedding. Theirs had been a business merger rather than a great love affair. Hell, she'd known Flint for most of her life, given that her socialite parents moved in influential LA circles and Flint was her dad's best friend. When Flint hinted at needing a wife to boost his profile and cement his position in Hollywood, Allegra had done what she did best. Help.

She'd been a helper her whole life, from tutoring fellow students lagging behind in class to tending wounded birds. From saving tables for the nerds in the cafeteria at high school to filling in at the college newspaper despite hating it. No great surprise why she did it, having no support from her parents whatsoever growing up and having to fend for herself. She valued her independence but seemed determined not to see others feel the same abandonment she had.

In the end, it looked like Flint hadn't wanted her help. And she'd been glad. She'd loved him in her own way, the kind of love for a good, reliable friend who would never let her down. They'd had a nice relationship, comfortable.

Which is why she'd agreed to a drink with the cocky, pushy Aussie.

She liked how he'd flirted: confident and teasing, with a killer sense of humor. She admired his boldness. It made her wish she could be more like him, and for the first time in a long time she'd felt something…a spark of attraction, a buzz in her belly, a twinge lower.

Damn, it felt good.

She rarely dated before Flint, had spent all her time building up AW Advertising from scratch before their three-year relationship began. Which meant she was thirty and hadn't mastered the art of flirting, let alone felt that buzz too often. The Aussie made her want to experience both.

The waiter deposited their drinks in front of her and she paid, wondering if she should drink fast and make a run for it. All these thoughts of flirting and buzzing were a frivolous waste of time, considering she wouldn't see the hottie again after they had a drink together.

The sound of soft female laughter farther along the bar drew her attention, as she watched a sultry brunette place her hand on a guy's thigh, lean in closer, and whisper something in his ear. Not surprisingly, the guy slid an arm around her waist, hugged her close, and planted a hot, open-mouthed kiss on her crimson-glossed lips.

A stab of jealousy speared Allegra as she turned away. She'd love to be that confident in her sexuality, that empowered to make a move and not analyze it to death.

"I'm officially nuts," she muttered under her breath, absentmindedly stirring her G&T with a straw.

Where did she think this could go? Fifteen minutes of

flirtation before they went their separate ways? Yep, definitely nuts.

"Hope you're practicing to whisper sweet nothings in my ear," he said, his warm breath fanning the tender skin beneath her earlobe and sending an unexpected shiver of longing through her.

Disconcerted by her physical reaction to him, especially since didn't know his name yet, she tilted her chin. "I don't whisper in the ears of strangers," she said, her abruptness making him chuckle.

"Is that your subtle way of asking my name?" He held out his hand. "Jett Halcott. Sydney-sider and proud of it."

"Allegra Wilks." She placed her hand in his and as his warm fingers curled over hers, another zing of electricity zapped her in places that were in serious need of zapping.

"I know." He held her hand a fraction too long—not that she was complaining.

"Know what?"

"Your name." He released her hand. "Saw it on your case."

"I'm surprised you didn't use it to your advantage."

"Didn't need to." He picked up his beer off the bar and raised it in her direction. "You're here, aren't you?"

She chuckled, unable to resist his teasing. There was something infinitely attractive about sharing a drink with a transient stranger, something exciting with a hint of daring. Far removed from her usual life.

"You should do that more often," he said, reaching out to trace her bottom lip with his fingertip. "You're beautiful, but when you smile? Wow."

Uncomfortable with his overt compliments, Allegra sat there and let a guy she'd just met touch her lips with a slow, sensual caress. His fingertip traced her bottom lip in a butterfly-soft sweep that left her breathless.

Their eyes locked as he lowered his hand, and what she saw made her wish she could ditch Palm Bay and travel to Australia.

Blatant lust. Strong. Sexy. Seductive. His eyes deepened to an incredible green that matched a favorite jade pendant she wore often. He wanted her, and in this crazy moment, the feeling was entirely mutual.

He raised his beer to his lips and took a long swig, his heat-filled stare never leaving hers.

Damn, she had no idea what to do in this situation.

Make a joke to diffuse the tension? Acknowledge it? Flirt?

She hated feeling out of control, had instigated steps her entire life to avoid it. Yet in a loaded thirty seconds, Jett had made her damp with just one look and made her flounder.

"Is the blatant charm an Aussie thing or is it just you?"

Thankfully, he blinked, and broke the scorching stare that made her want to grab a napkin off the bar and fan herself. "It's me." He leaned in close. "Time you fessed up."

Yikes. Was her reaction to him that easy to read?

"To what?"

His lips almost brushed her ear. "You're battling an incredible urge to drag me into the nearest janitor's closet and ravish me."

She laughed at his outrageousness. "Sorry. I don't do sex in cleaning closets. Too many hazardous chemicals."

"Yeah, those pheromones can be killer."

She loved his quick wit and for the second time in as many minutes, wished she'd met him at a different place, different time.

"Pity." He reverted to a smoldering stare that had her

wishing she'd ordered a vodka shot chaser. "Sex in confined spaces can be fun."

"I'll take your word for it." Heat crept into her cheeks and she signaled the waiter for a glass of water.

To douse herself with.

"Not the answer I was hoping for," he said, shifting his barstool closer so their thighs brushed. "Would've been better if you'd said, 'Sounds good, Jett, let's go try.'"

She cleared her throat and gratefully accepted the water from the waiter, drinking it all and wishing she could run the cool beaded exterior across her forehead.

"How did we get onto this crazy topic?"

"Started with you wanting to ravish me." He clinked his beer bottle to her empty glass. "Seriously.

There's no need to hold back. I can take whatever you want to dish out."

Oh, boy.

She could blame her lightheadedness on the alcohol, but she'd be lying. Thankfully, he reined in his overpowering masculinity to drain his beer, giving her an unimpeded view of his throat and the tanned skin there. Her fingers itched with the urge to touch…

"Hate to cut this short but…" He glanced at his watch and grimaced. "I have a plane to catch."

Ridiculous regret tempered her uncharacteristic yearning to spend five more minutes in his company.

"Me, too."

"Shame, really." He held out his hand to help her off the barstool, and while she didn't need it, she took it anyway. "We could've had some fun together."

For the first time in her life, Allegra couldn't agree more.

Maybe it was the shock of having her groom dump her

hours before the wedding, maybe it was years of rigid self-control, maybe it was the simple fact that she'd never experienced the gut-twisting attraction buzzing between her and Jett, but what she was feeling now?

Reckless and impulsive and crazy. Crazy enough to kiss a stranger good-bye.

She stared at his mouth, imagined what it would feel like on hers.

"Whatever you're thinking, I like it," he said, tugging on her hand and pulling her in close.

"This is insane," she said, a second before she kissed him, snatching her hand out of his so she could slide her arms around his waist and grope his butt.

Oh wow...firm...sexy...ass... were the only things that registered as he deepened the kiss, angling her head, his tongue sweeping into her mouth with commanding precision.

She made an embarrassing needy sound in her throat, partway between a gasp and a moan, and he drew her to him, the heat from his body making her meld to him.

The dampness he'd elicited earlier with a look turned into so much more when his hard-on pressed against her. To her utter shock, she was on the verge of coming.

With Flint it had taken a good ten minutes of foreplay for her to feel remotely turned on, and even then it wasn't a guarantee of an orgasm. How could this stranger have her desperate to rub against him in the hope of getting off?

Hoots and a wolf whistle filtered through her lust-filled haze and brought her back to reality. She wrenched her mouth from his, pressed her palms against his chest—whoa, nice pecs—and pushed. He didn't budge.

"Ignore them, they're just jealous," he said, his voice

husky as he stared at her lips. "You pack a helluva bon voyage kiss."

Heat surged to her cheeks, and this time when she pushed against his chest he released her.

She didn't want to discuss the kiss or acknowledge how she yearned to ditch Palm Bay and follow him Down Under.

Damn. Bad analogy, considering she still buzzed *down there* in a big way.

His lips quirked into a wicked smile that made her think of long, hot, sultry nights spent naked and sweaty and entwined. "I'm guessing you don't do long distance?"

She stared at him in disbelief. "One kiss and you want a relationship?"

"Babe, you misunderstood." He trailed a fingertip along her jaw, lingering just below her mouth, where her lips still tingled. "Long-distance means phone sex."

This time, the heat from her cheeks seeped southward. She'd never done phone sex, yet there was something about Jett that made her want to try.

She could imagine listening to that lazy Aussie drawl murmuring dirty words, telling her how to touch herself while he jerked off...

Damn. Not helping.

"How about it?" He leaned in close to murmur in her ear. "Wouldn't you like to get hot and bothered without an audience next time?"

What she'd like is to get extremely hot and bothered, but with him present, not on the end of some stupid phone. Considering they'd never see each other again, she summoned the bravado to tell him.

"What I'd really like..." She slid her hand around the back of his neck and lowered his head so her lips grazed his ear. "You and me. Naked. Having hot and sweaty, unforgettable, wild, climb-the-walls sex."

"Fuck," he said, turning his head a fraction to claim her lips again.

With her body straining toward him and her panties so damp she'd have to change into one of those mortifyingly skimpy things Zoe had packed, she put every ounce of yearning into the kiss. Not surprised at her sigh of disappointment when they eased apart.

"I have to go," she said, grabbing her suitcase handle and making a run for it before she changed her mind.

As she strode away on wobbly legs without looking back, she wanted him to come after her. She wanted him to take her up on the brazen offer she'd thrown out, knowing full well he couldn't.

She wanted him. Period.

But he didn't come after her and she didn't look back. And for one, insane moment she thought her wishful imagination had conjured up a murmured "see you soon" from the guy who'd made her lose control for the first time in forever.

∼

Jett hadn't played fair. Screw it. Life wasn't fair. He'd learned that the hard way.

Allegra would learn the truth soon enough.

Besides, he wanted to see her priceless expression when he sauntered into that first-class cabin and sat next to her.

It had taken some quick finagling and a hefty sum to upgrade from business to first, but if Allegra's departing comment was anything to go by, it'd be worth it.

He'd never met anyone like her. Fire and ice. Passion and aloofness. Hot and cold.

He planned on unleashing that heat. Soon.

For a guy who'd done the rounds and dated his fair share of women, he'd never had mile-high action. Guys in the surf crowd had boasted about it back in Bondi but he often wondered how much of their big talk was fact or fiction. Guys spun shit the way girls liked to shop. Natural as breathing.

But the thought of having sex with Allegra on a plane had him harder than a horny teen, if that were possible. As for the unexpected bonus of having her travel to his all-important destination… While nailing the business deal on Palm Bay was imperative, he could definitely do with a little R & R of the sizzling variety.

Her spontaneous kiss had been unexpected and her bold declaration had cemented what he'd suspected. The chemistry they had going on would equate to sensational sex. Which they would definitely have. If she didn't throw him out the emergency door without a parachute when she learned he'd withheld the pertinent information of his destination.

He knew how this would go: she'd be angry and would freeze him out for a while. But he'd faced bigger challenges, and after the way she'd almost combusted in his arms…

Oh yeah, this flight to Palm Bay would far exceed expectations and take the edge off the relentless disappointment that had dogged him since he'd learned the truth about his best mate and business partner.

If Jett hadn't made a few wise investments away from their business, he'd now be broke. Without a cent to claw his way back. And clawing his way back was exactly what he intended on doing, starting with landing the lucrative Kaluna Resorts campaign.

He'd almost lost everything when Reeve had fleeced their company. Lost his dignity, his cash, and his reputation in an industry where he'd been on top for years. Landing Kai Kaluna would go a long way to restoring his professional name. And prove to everyone, including his dad, that no one or nothing could stop him.

He shouldn't have splurged on upgrading his airline ticket—who knew how much of his personal cash stash he'd need to use to fund his new advertising company?—but he'd had enough shitty luck lately to last a lifetime, and the prospect of a little recreation of the horizontal kind with Allegra called for drastic measures.

Worth every cent to be holed up with her in a private first-class compartment with the airline's specialty romance package thrown in. It was also guaranteed to change his luck.

He gave Allegra a good five minutes' head start, and waited until she'd boarded before following at a sedate pace. As he handed over his boarding pass, walked along the airbridge, and smiled at the flight attendant welcoming him aboard, he wished he'd had time to make a stop at the pharmacy. That one condom in his wallet wouldn't be nearly enough for an eight-hour flight and what he wanted to do with Allegra.

∽

Allegra relaxed into the butter-soft cream leather of her first-class seat and sighed. She often traveled business class for work, but the compartment Flint had booked on this commercial flight made that look like coach on a budget airline.

She loved the wide armchair, with enough legroom to stretch, wiggle her toes, and hit nothing. And a flat-screen TV promised a host of nonstop, top-notch entertainment for the flight. But the best feature was a sliding door, ensuring privacy from the rest of the privileged passengers.

The only thing she didn't like was the matching empty seat beside her.

She'd heard about these first-class compartments on the latest whiz-bang planes. Privacy assured, with seats that converted into a queen-size bed. No surprise that Flint had booked it for their honeymoon. It fit with his high profile: everything done with practiced extravagance.

A sliver of sorrow pierced her pragmatism as she wondered what it would be like to share this intimate space with someone important. She'd thought that person would be Flint, but it wasn't to be. Guess she should be grateful he hadn't canceled the seat before the devastating call from her farm client had come through and she'd had to utilize it anyway.

"Champagne, madam?"

Allegra smiled her thanks at the flight attendant as she accepted a flute. "Yes, please."

She needed a drink. Fast. Needed something to take the edge off. Sadly, as she sipped the expensive champagne and the bubbles tickled her throat, she knew an alcohol injection wouldn't ease what was bugging her.

Damn that cocky Aussie.

Even now, fifteen minutes since she'd walked away from him and boarded the plane, she couldn't forget the buzz. The way he'd teased her. Held her. Kissed her. Damn, she wanted more. With a ferocity that defied logic.

Sex with Flint had been nice. Yet in less than five minutes at that bar, Jett had made her want to rip her clothes off, shove him against the nearest wall, and clamber all over him.

Which made her wonder. Had she sold herself short in accepting a lackluster sex life in exchange for a stable relationship with infinite business possibilities? At the time she'd thought it had been sensible to marry for friendship and work. Had pretended Flint's staid, bordering-on-repressed antics in the bedroom didn't bother her. Lights out, missionary position, once a week like clockwork, had seemed a small price to pay for a Hollywood marriage made in heaven.

But that kiss with Jett had proved she'd been delusional, her tingling skin from rubbing against Jett's deliciously hard body taunting her to admit the truth: that putting her business first may be financially and professionally rewarding, but it made for a lousy bedfellow.

What she wouldn't have given to have half an hour in bed with Jett...

Maybe she should've given him her number for a little of that phone sex action he'd mentioned after all?

She downed the rest of her champagne in three gulps at the thought.

This crazy, out-of-control feeling had to be a result of stress, and as she glanced at the empty first-class seat in the exclusive cabin Flint had booked, guilt pierced her faint alcohol buzz.

She should be more upset their wedding had been called off. She shouldn't be lusting after a stranger she'd had a chance encounter with. Yet here she was, not particularly heartbroken that her ex-fiancé wasn't accompanying her to the luxurious Palm Bay, and still unable to get Jett out of her head.

Had her priorities been so screwed up that even at this point, she was more concerned about scoring an opportunity to present her pitch to Kai Kaluna than what her friends and family would think about her aborted wedding?

Flint had said he'd take care of everything. And he had, issuing a press release to all the major Hollywood gossip mags this morning, accompanied by a trumped up photo of him and a voluptuous brunette cozying up at a recent film premiere. Along with a brief statement that his engagement to prominent, successful advertising guru Allegra Wilks was over.

The paparazzi had gone wild.

"Hollywood Heartbreak" and *"Producer on the Prowl"* had been some of the tamer headlines. Flint had laughed over the wildly inaccurate speculation in the press when they'd chatted on the phone and she'd berated him for deliberately taking the fall.

It shouldn't have surprised her. Flint was old school Hollywood, a gentleman through and through.

The only people who knew the truth were her parents. No way would she be responsible for their long-standing friendship suffering, so she'd sat down with them and Flint an hour after he'd called off the wedding and explained.

Daphne and Ross Wilks, Beverly Hills royalty, hadn't been impressed. Yet they'd cheered up pretty damn quick when they heard Flint would foot the exorbitant cancellation fees and take care of everything else.

Not once did her parents ask how she was feeling.

Not once did her mom commiserate or offer chocolate or a hug.

Not once did they ask if she needed anything.

When was the last time they acknowledged her anyway? At birth? When she was a five-year-old being shipped off to boarding school? When they air-kissed her at graduation before leaving immediately after the ceremony to attend some gallery opening?

Not surprising she overcompensated by offering assistance to everyone, whether they needed it or not.

She'd accepted their narcissistic parenting a long time ago, had learned to don a nonchalant mask as if nothing they did or said bothered her. But it did, and her blasé attitude soon spilled into all areas of her life.

She'd heard what employees said about her behind her back: detached, cool, Ice Queen.

She didn't care. Being a boss—and a damn generous one at that—demanded that she maintain a distance from her workers. Made for better production, rather than being buddy-buddy, knowing their firstborn's name or which basketball team they supported.

Oddly enough, it was the descriptions of her in the media during her engagement that bothered her most: indifferent, dispassionate, apathetic. They'd made her sound cold and heartless, criticizing everything from her clothes to her hair, when all she'd ever done was try to appear elegant and cool in public because of Flint's high profile. Flint had insisted it was par for the course, that everyone in the Hollywood limelight copped it. She'd accepted it, but she hadn't liked it. Liked less the fact that there was an element of truth in the crap they printed.

She did feel cold inside. Untouchable. Like no one could broach the brittle veneer she'd constructed to protect herself a long time ago. Yet in fifteen minutes, Jett Halcott, with a wicked twinkle in his eyes and a decadent smile, had warmed her in a way she'd never thought possible.

"Is this seat available?"

The champagne flute slipped from her fingers and fell to the carpet as she stared in disbelief at the guy she'd been fantasizing about.

"What the hell are you doing here?"

"I'll take that as a yes." He sat and grinned at her like it was the most natural thing in the world for him to be here. "Miss me?"

Wishing she hadn't had the champagne to cloud her brain, she shook her head and immediately regretted it when everything in her orbit spun. "You didn't answer my question."

"And you didn't answer mine." His forearm brushed hers on the armrest and she jumped. "I guess you just did."

"I'd have to care to miss you," she said, tilting her nose a fraction in the air, spoiling her act when his fingers deliberately grazed her wrist and she sighed.

"You care," he said, tracing a circle over her pulse point and sending a shudder of longing through her. "I intend to prove how much by the end of this flight."

She snatched her hand away and tried to drag up some righteous indignation. "You knew you were on this flight and you didn't tell me?"

He shrugged, infuriatingly smug. "What's there to tell? We shared a drink at the bar, now we'll share...a few more here."

His deliberate pause led her to believe he wanted to share a lot more besides drinks. Oh no...that's the second she remembered the very last thing she'd said to him. A feisty challenge thrown out in the heat of the moment to a stranger she'd never see again.

You and me. Naked. Having hot and sweaty, unforgettable, wild, climb-the-walls sex.

By the lascivious gleam in his green-eyed gaze, she wasn't the only one who remembered.

She was so busted.

"We'll be taking off soon." She gestured at the other first-class compartments. "Shouldn't you get back to your seat?"

She knew his response before he spoke, as his lips curved into a taunting smirk.

"This is my seat."

Eight hours in a private compartment with him?

Allegra didn't know whether to punch him for orchestrating this, or jump him.

"Your seat shouldn't have been available." She glared at him through narrowed eyes, reverting to type, not wanting him to see how seriously rattled she was by his appearance. And the fact that these seats could convert to a big bed when the lights turned down. "How did you do it?"

He smirked. "You know that thing you have for my accent? Maybe the check-in girls weren't so immune to it, either."

She snorted. "Insufferable and cocky. Could there be a worse combination?"

"Vegemite and pavlova."

She bit back the urge to laugh at his humor.

"What?"

"You have heard of Vegemite and pav, right? Aussie icon foods?"

She had, but he was having so much fun in his righteous smugness she'd let him run with it. "Why don't you enlighten me?"

"Heathen," he said, his teasing smile doing weird things to her pulse. "Imagine a black, salty yeast paste. That's Vegemite."

She screwed up her nose, when in fact she'd tried it at a post-Oscars party once and loved it.

"And pavlova is a meringue-based, cream-filled dessert topped with fresh fruit or chocolate crumbs."

Yum. "Your point?"

"You asked about bad combinations, I just gave you one." He winked. "Pity. I thought you were more than just a pretty face."

She would've puffed up in outrage, considering that he'd implied she was stupid, if she hadn't seen the amusement deepening his eyes to moss, and a hint of something more. Uncertainty. For all his bluster, the Aussie hadn't been sure of his reception. Had maybe expected her to be pissed off he hadn't told her his destination when they'd had a drink earlier.

And damn, if that glimmer of doubt didn't make her like him all the more.

"Don't be obtuse," she said, with a toss of her hair, enjoying the instant flare of heat in his eyes as a few strands brushed his arm.

"Don't use big words," he said, snagging the strands, rubbing them between his fingers, before winding them around his index finger and tugging gently.

Her scalp prickled at the delicious sensation as she clamped down on the urge to grab his hand and shove a whole fistful of her hair into it.

"Must add deprecating to your many talents," she said, her dry response garnering another gentle tug as he wound her hair tighter.

"You have no idea how talented I really am."

With one more wind his hand reached her head, his fingertips gliding along her scalp in a slow caress that made her melt in a puddle of longing.

She should rebuke him, should set the record straight about that flyaway sex remark before she'd boarded. But she couldn't think, not with his fingers delving through her hair. How could a simple scalp massage be so damn erotic?

Her eyelids fluttered shut and her head lolled back as she savored the incredible sensation of having a guy who wasn't her hairdresser play with her hair.

"Excuse me, we're taking off shortly." The flight attendant cleared her throat. "Can I have your empty glass, please?"

Allegra's eyelids snapped open to find the flight attendant regarding her with open envy as Jett brushed his knuckles against her cheek before straightening.

"Uh, yeah, sure." Allegra handed over the glass, not surprised her hand trembled. "Thanks."

"I'm sure you'll both have a pleasant flight," the flight attendant said, beaming before she moved on to the next compartment.

"I'm sure we will, too." Jett's heated gaze locked on hers, daring her to disagree.

Allegra couldn't. Not when her scalp still tingled and her body was burning up from the inside out.

Eight hours on a plane, in a private compartment, with a sexy Aussie.

Nope, she wouldn't dare disagree.

To read on, buy WICKED HEAT and the sequel WANTON HEAT, out now!

With her reputation on the line, reformed bad-girl Zoe Keaton heads to Italy to score a vital business deal.

Unfortunately, the guy she needs to convince is the wickedly hot—and totally closed-off—Prince Dominic Ricci.

When the queen's matchmaking strands Zoe and the prince on the royal family's secluded island, Zoe vows not to mix business with pleasure.

But the prince turns up the heat, and the chemistry between them ignites. Is it just sizzling sex, or could an Italian prince with a tragic past fall for a take-no-prisoners American?

BUY WANTON HEAT!

ABOUT THE AUTHOR

USA TODAY bestselling and multi-award winning author Nicola Marsh writes page-turning fiction to keep you up all night.
She's published 82 books and sold 8 million copies worldwide.
She currently writes contemporary romance and domestic suspense.
She's also a Waldenbooks, Bookscan, Amazon, iBooks and Barnes & Noble bestseller, a RBY (Romantic Book of the Year) and National Readers' Choice Award winner, and a multi-finalist for a number of awards including the Romantic Times Reviewers' Choice Award, HOLT Medallion, Booksellers' Best, Golden Quill, Laurel Wreath, and More than Magic.
A physiotherapist for thirteen years, she now adores writing full time, raising her two dashing young heroes, sharing fine food with family and friends, and her favorite, curling up with a good book!